THE SECRET GARDEN

Book and Lyrics
by Marsha Norman

Music by Lucy Simon

based on the novel by Frances Hodgson Burnett

SAMUEL FRENCH, INC.

45 West 25th Street   NEW YORK 10010

7623 Sunset Boulevard   HOLLYWOOD 90046

LONDON   *TORONTO*

◪ ST. JAMES THEATRE

A JUJAMCYN THEATRE

JAMES H. BINGER
CHAIRMAN

ROCCO LANDESMAN
PRESIDENT

PAUL LIBIN
PRODUCING DIRECTOR

JACK VIERTEL
CREATIVE DIRECTOR

Heidi Landesman

Rick Steiner, Frederic H. Mayerson, Elizabeth Williams,
Jujamcyn Theaters / TV ASAHI and Dodger Productions

present

Book and Lyrics by   Music by
Marsha Norman   **Lucy Simon**
based on the novel by Frances Hodgson Burnett

with

(in alphabetical order)
John Babcock   **Daisy Eagan**   **Alison Fraser**
Rebecca Luker   **John Cameron Mitchell**   **Mandy Patinkin**
Barbara Rosenblat   **Tom Toner**   **Robert Westenberg**

Michael De Vries   **Paul Jackel**   **Nancy Johnston**
Rebecca Judd   **Kimberly Mahon**   **Peter Marinos**
Patricia Phillips   **Peter Samuel**   **Drew Taylor**   **Kay Walbye**

Teresa De Zarn   **Frank Di Pasquale**   **Betsy Friday**   **Alec Timerman**

Scenery by
Heidi Landesman

Costumes by
Theoni V. Aldredge

Lighting by
Tharon Musser

Orchestrations by
William D. Brohn

Musical Direction and
Vocal Arrangements
Michael Kosarin

Dance
Arrangements
Jeanine Levenson

Sound by
Otts Munderloh

Choreography by
Michael Lichtefeld

Casting
Wendy Ettinger

Production Stage Manager
Perry Cline

Musical Coordinator
John Miller

Hair and Makeup Design by
Robert DiNiro

General Management
David Strong Warner, Inc.

Production Manager
Peter Fulbright

Press Representation
Adrian Bryan-Brown

Directed by
Susan H. Schulman

Senior Associate Producer
Greg C. Mosher
Associate Producers
Rhoda Mayerson   Dentsu Inc. New York   Dorothy and Wendell Cherry
Margo Lion   126 Second Ave. Corp.   Playhouse Square Center

Originally produced by Virginia Stage Company, Charles Towers, Artistic Director.
The Producers and Theatre Management are members of The League of American Theaters and Producers, Inc.
The Producers wish to express their appreciation to Theatre Development Fund for its support of this production.

CAST

Lily .... REBECCA LUKER
Mary Lennox .... DAISY EAGAN
Mary Lennox (Wed. Mats. and Thurs. Eves.) .... KIMBERLY MAHON

IN COLONIAL INDIA, 1906:

Fakir .... PETER MARINOS
Ayah .... PATRICIA PHILLIPS
Rose (Mary's mother) .... KAY WALBYE
Captain Albert Lennox (Mary's father) .... MICHAEL De VRIES
Lieutenant Peter Wright .... DREW TAYLOR
Lieutenant Ian Shaw .... PAUL JACKEL
Major Holmes .... PETER SAMUEL
Claire (his wife) .... REBECCA JUDD
Alice (Rose's friend) .... NANCY JOHNSTON

AT MISSELTHWAITE MANOR, NORTH YORKSHIRE, ENGLAND, 1906:

Archibald Craven (Mary's uncle) .... MANDY PATINKIN
Dr. Neville Craven (his brother) .... ROBERT WESTENBERG
Mrs. Medlock (the housekeeper) .... BARBARA ROSENBLAT
Martha (a chambermaid) .... ALISON FRASER
Dickon (her brother) .... JOHN CAMERON MITCHELL
Ben (the gardener) .... TOM TONER
Colin .... JOHN BABCOCK
Jane .... TERESA De ZARN
William .... FRANK DiPASQUALE
Betsy .... BETSY FRIDAY
Timothy .... ALEC TIMERMAN
Mrs. Winthrop (the headmistress) .... NANCY JOHNSTON

ALL OTHER PARTS ARE PLAYED BY THE ENSEMBLE

UNDERSTUDIES

Understudies never substitute for listed players unless a specific announcement
for the appearance is made at the time of the performance.

Alternate for Mary Lennox — KIMBERLY MAHON
Standby for Archibald Craven — GREG ZERKLE

For Lily — TERESA De ZARN, NANCY JOHNSTON; for Mary Lennox — MELODY
KAY; for Archibald Craven — MICHAEL De VRIES, PETER SAMUEL; for Dr. Neville
Craven — MICHAEL De VRIES, PAUL JACKEL; for Mrs. Medlock — REBECCA JUDD,
JANE SEAMAN; for Martha — BETSY FRIDAY, JENNIFER SMITH; for Dickon —
KEVIN LIGON, ALEC TIMERMAN; for Ben — BILL NOLTE, DREW TAYLOR; for
Colin — JOEL E. CHAIKEN; for Rose — TERESA De ZARN, BETSY FRIDAY; for Cap-
tain Albert Lennox — PAUL JACKEL, GREG ZERKLE; for Fakir — KEVIN LIGON,
ALEC TIMERMAN; for Ayah — REBECCA JUDD, JENNIFER SMITH; for Lieutenant
Peter Wright—FRANK DiPASQUALE, BILL NOLTE; for Lieutenant Ian Shaw—KEVIN
LIGON, ALEC TIMERMAN; for Major Holmes—FRANK DiPASQUALE, BILL NOLTE;
for Claire—BETSY FRIDAY, JANE SEAMAN; for Alice—BETSY FRIDAY, JENNIFER
SMITH; for Mrs. Winthrop — REBECCA JUDD, JENNIFER SMITH.

SWINGS: KEVIN LIGON, BILL NOLTE, JANE SEAMAN, JENNIFER SMITH

SYNOPSIS OF SCENES

ACT I

Opening:

"Opening Dream".............................. Lily, Fakir, Mary & Company
              India
"There's a Girl" ....Company
              The Library at Misselthwaite Manor
              A Train Platform in Yorkshire
              The Door to Misselthwaite Manor
"The House Upon the Hill"..Company
              Mary's Room
              The Gallery
"I Heard Someone Crying" ....Mary, Archibald, Lily & Company

Scene 1:   **Mary's Sitting Room**
"A Fine White Horse" .... Martha

Scene 2:   **The Ballroom**
"A Girl in the Valley" .... Lily, Archibald & Dancers

Scene 3:   **In the Maze/The Greenhouse**
"It's a Maze .... Ben, Mary, Dickon & Martha
              The Edge of the Moor
"Winter's on the Wing"..Dickon
"Show Me the Key" ....Mary & Dickon

Scene 4:   **Archibald's Library**
"A Bit of Earth" ....Archibald

Scene 5:   **The Gallery**
"Storm I" ....Company
"Lily's Eyes" ....Archibald & Neville

Scene 6:   **The Hallway**
"Storm II" ....Mary & Company

Scene 7:   **Colin's Room**
"Round-Shouldered Man" ....Colin

Scene 8:   **On the Grounds / The Door to the Garden**
"Final Storm" ....Company

ACT II

CHARACTERS

LILY – Mary's aunt, Mr. Craven's wife, now dead.
MARY LENNOX – a ten-year-old girl.
MRS. MEDLOCK – Mr. Craven's housekeeper.
DR. NEVILLE CRAVEN – Mr. Craven's brother.
MARTHA – a housemaid.
ARCHIBALD CRAVEN – Mary's uncle, and lord of Misselthwaite Manor.
BEN WEATHERSTAFF – head gardener.
DICKON – Martha's brother.
COLIN CRAVEN – Archibald Craven's ten-year-old son.
MRS. WINTHROP – headmistress.

*DREAMERS:
ROSE LENNOX – Mary's mother.
CAPTAIN ALBERT LENNOX – Mary's father.
ALICE – Rose's friend.
LIEUTENANT WRIGHT – officer in Mary's father's unit.
LIEUTENANT SHAW – fellow officer.
MAJOR SHELLEY – officer.
MRS. SHELLEY – Major Shelley's wife.
MAJOR HOLMES – officer.
CLAIRE HOLMES – Major Holmes' wife.
FAKIR
AYAH – Mary's Indian nanny.

*These characters, referred to collectively as the Dreamers, are people from Mary's life in India, who haunt her until she finds her new life in the course of this story. They are free to sing directly to us, appearing and disappearing at will.

TIME & PLACE

1906. Colonial India and
Misselthwaite Manor, North Yorkshire, England.

THE SECRET GARDEN
ACT I
PROLOGUE

[MUSIC CUE #1: PRELUDE]

Behind a scrim, a beautiful young WOMAN, dressed in white, sits in the branch of a large old tree. MARY LENNOX, a ten-year-old girl, is seen playing with a Victorian doll's house.

[MUSIC CUE #2: OPENING]

LILY. (*As LILY sings, MARY hums.*)
CLUSTERS OF CROCUS,
PURPLE AND GOLD.
BLANKETS OF PANSIES,
UP FROM THE COLD.
LILIES AND IRIS,
SAFE FROM THE CHILL.
SAFE IN MY GARDEN,
SNOWDROPS SO STILL.

(An Indian FAKIR appears and begins to chant.)

FAKIR.
AH ...
A'O JADU KE MAUSAM.
A'O GARMIYO KE DIN.
A'O MANTRA TANTRA YANTRA,
US KI BIMARI, HATA 'O

AH ...
A'O JADU KE MAUSAM.
A'O GARMIYO KE DIN.

9

A'O MANTRA TANTRA YANTRA,
US KI BIMARI, HATA' O.

(Mary's father, ALBERT, enters, carries her to an ornate Victorian bed, center stage, and kisses her goodnight. As she goes to sleep, he steps back and English COUPLES appear, as if in a dream, around the bed.
At *ALBERT'S salute, the COUPLES begin to play* DROP THE HANDKERCHIEF *using a red handkerchief. Those present include: ROSE, Mary's mother, a beautiful woman who seems to be flirting with all the men, ALBERT, Mary's father, ALICE, Rose's friend, two lieutenants, WRIGHT and SHAW, serving the Raj in colonial India, MAJOR HOLMES and his wife, CLAIRE, and a FAKIR, and Mary's AYAH.*
The echo of children's voices is heard.)

CHILDREN'S VOICES.
MISTRESS MARY, QUITE CONTRARY,
HOW DOES YOUR GARDEN GROW?
NOT SO WELL, SHE SAID, SEE THE LILY'S DEAD.
PULL IT UP AND OUT YOU GO.

(As the game proceeds, we realize the players are not merely eliminated from the game, but have, in fact, died of the cholera in Colonial India. One by one, they take out red handkerchiefs and dab at their faces and necks.)

CHILDREN'S VOICES.
MISTRESS MARY, QUITE CONTRARY,
HOW DOES YOUR GARDEN GROW?
FAR TOO HOT, SHE CRIED, SEE MY ROSE HAS DIED.
DIG IT UP, AND OUT YOU GO.

LOOK AROUND, LOOK AROUND, WHAT DO YOU
SEE?
PLANTS IN THE GROUND, ALL ARE BLIND TO
THEE.
WALK AROUND, WALK AROUND, WHERE WILL
YOU GO
SEEDS IN THE EARTH, COVERED UP WITH
SNOW.

MISTRESS MARY, QUITE CONTRARY,
HOW DOES YOUR GARDEN GROW?
OH IT'S DRY, SHE WAILED, SEE THE IRIS
FAILED,
PULL IT UP, AND OUT YOU GO.

MISTRESS MARY, QUITE CONTRARY, HOW DOES
YOUR GARDEN GROW?
HAD AN EARLY FROST, NOW IT'S GONE, IT'S
LOST.
DIG IT UP, YOU'RE OUT, YOU'RE UP, YOU'RE
OUT
YOU'RE UP, YOU'RE OUT, YOU GO ...

*(Finally, when no one is left alive, MARY awakes, as if
from a terrible dream, and then falls back, as mosquito
netting drops down over the bed.)*

INDIA

*(The next morning, MARY sits on her bed, looking at a
small photograph in a frame, and humming "Clusters
of Crocus."*
LT. WRIGHT *enters, his mouth covered with a
handkerchief. He hears the humming and discovers
MARY.)*

LIEUTENANT WRIGHT. (*Calling to someone
offstage.*) Major. There's a girl in here.

MAJOR. (*As he enters.*) Do you mean alive?

MARY. My name is Mary Lennox. Where has everyone gone? Where's my Ayah?

(*The MAJOR takes note of the girl, then looks around the room, careful of what he touches, as though everything might be contaminated.*)

LIEUTENANT WRIGHT. We've searched the servants' bungalow as well sir. It's just one blacksnake and this girl.

MARY. Why has no one come for me?

MAJOR HOLMES. I'm afraid there's no one left, Miss.

LIEUTENANT WRIGHT. Bloody miracle she escaped the cholera, though God knows how. She was drinkin' the same water they was.

MARY. But where are my mother and father?

MAJOR HOLMES. I'm sorry, Miss.

LIEUTENANT WRIGHT. Where shall I take the girl, sir? Our orders are to burn anything that might be contaminated.

MAJOR HOLMES. To Governor's house for now. I believe there's an uncle, somewhere.

LIEUTENANT WRIGHT. Yes, sir. You'll have to leave that picture here, miss.

MARY. No, I will not! I'm taking it with me.

LIEUTENANT WRIGHT. It's your pretty mother, is it?

MARY. No, it isn't.

LIEUTENANT WRIGHT. Yes, well. Come along then.

[MUSIC CUE # 3: THERE'S A GIRL–I]

(*MARY takes the small framed photo and puts it in her pocket. As they leave, the ornate dollhouse bursts into flames.*)

LIEUTENANT SHAW.
CAN IT BE A DREAM?
SURELY IT MUST SEEM
LIKE A FRIGHTFUL DREAM.
HOW CAN THIS BE TRUE?
LIEUTENANT WRIGHT and MAJOR HOLMES.
WON'T HER MOTHER COME,
COME WAKE HER UP TO PLAY?
WON'T HER FATHER SAY,
HERE'S A ROSE FOR YOU?
CLAIRE, ALICE, HOLMES and WRIGHT.
THERE'S A GIRL WHOM NO ONE SEES.
THERE'S A GIRL WHO'S LEFT ALONE.
THERE'S A HEART THAT BEATS IN SILENCE FOR
THE LIFE SHE'S NEVER KNOWN.
FOR THE LIFE SHE'S NEVER KNOWN.

A TRAIN PLATFORM IN YORKSHIRE

(MAJOR SHELLEY and his wife arrive with MARY.)

MRS. SHELLEY. She's such a sour young thing.
Perhaps if Rose had spent more time in the nursery, Mary
might have learned some of her mother's pretty ways.

(ROSE enters.)

MAJOR SHELLEY. What a nightmare it must have
been for the girl. To wander up to bed in the middle of a
party, then wake up the next morning with them all dead.

(MRS. MEDLOCK approaches.)

MRS. MEDLOCK. Good evening, Major. I'm Mr.
Craven's housekeeper. Is this the girl?

(ALBERT appears.)

MAJOR SHELLEY. Yes ma'am. And here's her papers and the death certificates and all. Her father was captain in my regiment and a fine man he was, too. We're all very sorry ...

MRS. MEDLOCK. Thank you, Major.

MAJOR HOLMES. Yes ma'am. A pleasant journey to you, mam.

MRS. MEDLOCK. (*Turns to MARY.*) Well, now. I suppose you'd like to know something about where you are going.

MARY. Would I.

MRS. MEDLOCK. But don't you care about your new home?

MARY. It doesn't matter whether I care or not.

MRS. MEDLOCK. Now in all my years, [MUSIC CUE #4: THE HOUSE UPON THE HILL] I've never seen a child sit so still or look so old.

DREAMERS.
HIGH ON A HILL SITS A BIG OLD HOUSE
WITH SOMETHING WRONG INSIDE IT.
SPIRITS HAUNT THE HALLS
AND MAKE NO EFFORT NOW TO HIDE IT.

WHAT WILL PUT THEIR SOULS TO REST
AND STOP THEIR CEASELESS SIGHING?
WHY DO THEY CALL OUT CHILDREN'S NAMES
AND SPEAK OF ONE WHO'S CRYING?

(*MRS. MEDLOCK continues talking, DREAMERS sing "OHH" under dialogue.*)

MRS. MEDLOCK. Well, you're right not to care. Why you're being brought to Misselthwaite I'll never know. Your uncle isn't going to trouble himself about you, that's sure and certain. He never troubles himself about anyone.

DREAMERS.
AND THE MASTER HEARS THE WHISPERS
ON THE STAIRWAYS DARK AND STILL,
AND THE SPIRITS SPEAK OF SECRETS
IN THE HOUSE UPON THE HILL.
MRS. MEDLOCK. He's a hunchback, you see.
And a sour young man he was, and got no good of all his
money and big place till he were married.

(LILY appears in a shaft of light.)

MARY. To my mother's sister?
MRS. MEDLOCK. Her name was Lily. And she
was a sweet, pretty thing and he'd have walked the world
over to get her a blade of grass that she wanted. Nobody
thought she'd marry him, but marry him she did, and it
wasn't for his money either. But then when she died ...
MARY. How did she die?
MRS. MEDLOCK. It made him worse than ever.
He travels most of the time now. It's his brother, Dr.
Craven, who makes all the decisions these days.
DREAMERS.
HIGH ON A HILL SITS A BIG OLD HOUSE
WITH SOMETHING WRONG INSIDE IT.
SOMEONE DIED AND SOMEONE'S LEFT
ALONE AND CAN'T ABIDE IT.

THERE IN THE HOUSE LIVES A LONELY MAN
STILL HAUNTED BY HER BEAUTY.
ASKING WHAT A LIFE CAN BE WHERE
WHERE NAUGHT REMAINS BUT DUTY.

(DREAMERS sing "OOH" under dialogue.)

MARY. Is it always so ugly here?
MRS. MEDLOCK. It's the moor. Miles and miles
of wild land that nothing grows on but heather and gorse

and broom, and nothing lives on but wild ponies and
sheep.

MARY. What is that awful howling sound?
MRS. MEDLOCK. That's the wind, blowing
through the bushes. They call it wuthering, that sound.
But look there, that tiny light far across there. That'll be
the gate it will.
DREAMERS.
AND THE MASTER HEARS THE WHISPERS
ON THE STAIRWAYS DARK AND STILL.
AND THE SPIRITS SPEAK OF SECRETS
IN THE HOUSE UPON THE HILL.

THE DOOR TO MISSELTHWAITE MANOR

*(ARCHIBALD and DR. CRAVEN meet just inside the
door, ARCHIBALD carrying a book, DR. CRAVEN
carrying a large candelabra.)*

DR. CRAVEN. For God's sake, Archie. The girl's
parents are dead. She's traveled six thousand miles to get
here. You *are* her guardian. The least you can do is be
here to greet her.
ARCHIBALD. I can't, Neville. I wouldn't know
what to say. *(Patting the book.)* I'll be upstairs.

*(ARCHIBALD exits, and the door opens and MARY and
MRS. MEDLOCK enter.)*

MRS. MEDLOCK. Mary Lennox, this is Dr.
Craven, your uncle's brother.
MARY. How do you do.
DR. CRAVEN. *(To MRS. MEDLOCK.)* You're to
take her to her room. He doesn't want to see her.
MRS. MEDLOCK. Very good, Doctor.

(MARY and MRS. MEDLOCK go into the house and up the stairs, as the DREAMERS appear and sing.)

[MUSIC CUE #5: THERE'S A GIRL–II]

MAJOR HOLMES and CLAIRE.
CAN IT BE A DREAM?
SURELY IT DOES SEEM
LIKE A FRIGHTFUL DREAM,
NO ONE HERE SHE KNOWS.
ALICE, LIEUTENANTS WRIGHT and SHAW.
SHADOWS ON THE WALLS,
DARK AND DRAFTY HALLS,
CATCH HER IF SHE FALLS,
STILL NO FEAR SHE SHOWS.

MARY'S ROOM

MRS. MEDLOCK. Well, here you are. This room and the next are where you'll live. But you mustn't expect that there will be people to talk to you. You'll have to play about and look after yourself. But when you're in the house, don't go wandering the halls. Your uncle won't have it.

MARY. *(As though asleep or in shock.)* ... won't have it.

(ROSE and ALBERT appear.)

ROSE. Albert, please ...
ALBERT. Rose, I really must send you and Mary away until we get this cholera under control.
ROSE. And what shall I do? Wander around the hills, alone with our child, while she stares at me the whole time.
ALBERT. She's not staring at you, Rose. Mary just wants to look at you. Just like all the rest of us.

MRS. MEDLOCK. (*Goes to the door.*) Goodnight, then.
  MARY. Yes, ma'am.

(MRS. MEDLOCK exits.)

  ALBERT.
THERE'S A GIRL WHOM NO ONE SEES.
THERE'S A GIRL WHO'S LEFT ALONE.
THERE'S A HEART THAT BEATS IN SILENCE FOR
THE LIFE SHE'S NEVER KNOWN.

  [MUSIC CUE #6: I HEARD SOMEONE CRYING]

*(LILY appears, and ALBERT extends his arm to her, as
    if asking her to take care of MARY.*
*But MARY can't sleep. She hears someone crying, picks
    up a candle and walks out into the house. As she
    sings, she sees someone rounding a corner and
    follows him. As she moves through the corridors, she
    continues to get glimpses of shadows, or ghosts from
    her past.*
LILY follows her.)

  LILY.
OOO ...
  MARY.
I HEARD SOMEONE CRYING.
WHO THO' COULD IT BE?
MAYBE IT WAS MOTHER
CALLING OUT, COME SEE
MAYBE IT WAS FATHER,
ALL ALONE, AND LOST AND COLD.
I HEARD SOMEONE CRYING.
MAYBE IT WAS ME ...

(MARY picks up a candle and goes into the gallery. ARCHIBALD appears in another part of the gallery with his candle.)

ARCHIBALD.
I HEARD SOMEONE SINGING.
WHO THO' COULD IT BE?
MAYBE IT WAS LILY,
CALLING OUT TO ME.
MAYBE SHE'S NOT GONE
SO FAR AWAY AS I'VE BEEN TOLD.
I HEARD SOMEONE SINGING.
MAYBE IT WAS SHE.

(Now MARY comes out of her hiding place, as ARCHIBALD moves into another part of the house.)

MARY.	**LILY.**
MAYBE IT WAS SOMEONE I COULD	OOO ...

FIND AND HAVE A CUP OF TEA.
MAYBE IT WAS SOMEONE WHO
COULD BRING THE TEA AND COME FIND ME.
   LILY.
I HEARD SOMEONE CRYING.
THO I CAN'T SAY WHO.
SOMEONE IN THIS HOUSE
WITH NOTHING LEFT TO DO.
SOUNDED LIKE A FATHER,
LEFT ALONE, HIS LOVE GROWN COLD.
I HEARD SOMEONE CRYING.
MAYBE IT WAS YOU.

(MARY holds her candle up to a large portrait of LILY.)

ARCHIBALD & MARY.
MAYBE I WAS DREAMING OF A GARDEN
   GROWING FAR BELOW

MAYBE I WAS DREAMING OF A LIFE THAT I WILL
    NEVER KNOW.

MARY/LILY	ARCHIBALD.
I HEARD SOMEONE CALLING.	LILY, WHERE ARE YOU, I'M LOST WITHOUT YOU
WHO THO' COULD IT BE?	I CAN'T WALK THESE HALLS WITHOUT YOU

MARY.	LILY.	ARCHIBALD.
SOMEONE IN THIS HOUSE	OOO ...	LILY, WHERE ARE YOU, I NEED YOU
WHOM NO ONE SEEMS TO SEE	OOO ...	I HAVE SEARCHED THE WORLD BUT YOU'RE NOT THERE
SOMEONE NO ONE SEEMED TO	OOO ...	COME AND TELL ME WHY YOU
HEAR EXCEPT FOR ME	OOO ...	BROUGHT ME HOME IF YOU'RE NOT HERE,

MARY / LILY.	ARCHIBALD.	DREAMERS
I HEARD SOMEONE CALLING	MY LILY, WHERE ARE YOU,	
	I'M LOST WITHOUT YOU	
SOMEONE IS CRYING	LILY, WHERE ARE YOU	LILY ......
	LILY, WHY CAN'T I FIND YOU	AH ......

MAYBE IT	FIND SOME	
WAS YOU	TRACE	
	YOU'VE LEFT	
	BEHIND YOU	
MAYBE ME	LILY, WHERE	
	ARE YOU	
	WITHOUT YOU, I	
	AM LOST	
I AM LOST	I AM LOST	I AM LOST

(ARCHIBALD and MARY blow out their candles.)

[MUSIC CUE #6A: I HEARD SOMEONE
CRYING–playoff]

SCENE 1
MARY'S SITTING ROOM

MARTHA, a sturdy Yorkshire girl, enters carrying a breakfast tray and a skipping rope.

[MUSIC CUE #6AA: MARTHA'S DITTY]

MARTHA.
ME MOTHER ASKED ME, LASSIE, TELL ME WHAT
YOUR LAD MUN DO
BEFORE YOU GIVE YOUR HEART AWAY, AND
MAKES A NEST, AND ALL THE REST.
I TOLD ME DARLIN' MOTHER THERE'S
SOMETHING HE MUN DO,
BUT I'LL SAY FIRST HOW HE MUN LOOK HIS
EYES, THEY BE MUN, TOO.
MARY. Are you my servant?

(Mary's AYAH appears.)

MARTHA. Well there, Mary Lennox. Me name is Martha. And now tha'rt up, I'll make tha' bed.

MARY. Aren't you going to dress me first?
MARTHA. Canna tha' dress thyself, then?

[MUSIC CUE #6B: INDIA STING #1]

MARY. In India, my Ayah dressed me.
MARTHA. Well then, it'll do tha' good to wait on
thysel' a bit. Tis fair a wonder grand folks children don't
turn out fair fools, bein' washed and took out to walk like
they was puppies.
MARY. *What* is this language you speak?
MARTHA. Well, of course, you've not heard any
Yorkshire, livin' in India, have ye? Mrs. Medlock said
I'd have to be careful or you wouldn't understand what I
was sayin'. But I didn't know what to expect from you
either. When I heard you was comin' from Bombay, I
thought you'd be a solid brown, I did. But you're not
brown at all. More yellow, I'd say.

*(MARY's hands fly up to her eyes, as she bursts into
tears and doesn't want MARTHA to see it.)*

MARTHA. Eh, now lassie, I didn't know you'd be
so easy vexed. I'll help you on with your clothes this
time, if you like. You just pretend you're back in India,
and I'm your servant, and you just give me that little
yellow foot.
MARY. I'm quite all right. Thank you.
MARTHA. Look there. Out the window. It's the
moor, it is. Like a dull purple sea this morning. Do you
like it?
MARY. I hate it.
MARTHA. Ah, you wait 'til spring, then. For the
moor is fair covered in gorse and heather, and there's
such a lot of fresh air. My brother Dickon goes off and
plays on the moor for hours. He's got a pony that's made
friends with him, and birds and sheep and such as eats
right out of his hand.

MARY. (*Has been examining the closet.*) These are not my clothes.

MARTHA. Ay, miss, your Uncle ...

MARY. (*Interrupting her to keep her from talking on and on.*) These are nicer than mine.

MARTHA. You get these new clothes on then, and wrap up warm and [MUSIC CUE #6C: MEDLOCK BELL#1] run out and play. That'll give you stomach for your porridge.

MARY. Mrs. Medlock told me there's nothing out there but a big old park.

MARTHA. Well, maybe you'll run into our Dickon out there. Maybe he'll give you a ride on his pony. Maybe he'll ...

MARY. I don't know anything about boys.

(*MARTHA sighs, and proceeds to dress MARY as she sings:*)

[MUSIC CUE #7: IF I HAD A FINE WHITE HORSE]

MARTHA.
IF I HAD A FINE WHITE HORSE,
I'D TAKE YOU FOR A RIDE TODAY.
BUT SINCE I HAVE NO FINE WHITE HORSE
INSIDE I'LL HAVE TO STAY,
    AND EMPTY ALL THE CHAMBER POTS
    AND SCRUB THE FLOORS AND SUCH.
BUT WHAT'S THERE TO DO ON A FINE WHITE
    HORSE?
IT SEEMS TO ME NOT MUCH.

IF I HAD A WOODEN BOAT,
I'D TAKE YOU FOR A SAIL TODAY.
BUT SINCE I HAVE NO WOODEN BOAT
INSIDE I'LL HAVE TO STAY
    AND CATCH AND KILL THE MICE,
    AND PLUCK THE CHICKENS FOR THE COOK.

BUT WHAT'S THERE TO DO ON A WOODEN BOAT,
BUT SIT UP STRAIGHT AND LOOK?

AND WORRY OUR BOAT WILL START TO DRIFT
AND FLOAT US OUT TO SEA ...
AND LAND US ON AN ISLE OF GOLD,
OH DEAR, OH DEARIE ME ...

IF I HAD A CHAMBER MAID,
I'D TAKE YOU OUT TO PLAY TODAY.
THEY SAY OUT THERE'S A MAZE WHERE
ONCE YOU ENTER, THERE YOU STAY.
FOR CERTAIN WE'D GET LOST AND THEY'D
    COME LOOKIN' FOR OUR BONES.
AND FIND US SOMETIME LATE NEXT WEEK
AND BRING US TEA AND SCONES.

          BUT WHAT IF THERE'S A CLAN OF
          TROLLS A CAMPIN' NEATH A TREE?
          OR WHAT IF THERE'S A PIRATES' CAVE,
          OH DEAR OH DEAR OH DEARIE ME ....

IF I WASN'T SO AFRAID,
I'D TAKE YOU OUT THE DOOR TODAY.
BUT TALKING BIRDS AND TALES OF FAIRIES
    KEEP ME SCARED AWAY.
AND YES, I PROMISED NOT TO TELL WHAT
ELSE IS THERE, ALTHOUGH ...
IF IN THE MAZE YOU CHANCE TO SEE
    A GARDEN GUARDED BY A TREE,
    AND MEET A BIRD THAT SPEAKS TO THEE ...
THEN COME AND TELL MY FINE WHITE HORSE
    AND ME

          [MUSIC CUE #7A: MEDLOCK BELL #2]

(MARY is all dressed now. MARTHA hears a BELL ringing.)

MARTHA. Oh, now there's Mrs. Medlock's bell, and I've got all this to clean up first. Can you find your way out yourself? It's down the stairs, past the ballroom...

MARY. I'll find it.

MARTHA. (*Picks up the skipping rope.*) Mary Lennox. I thought tha' might like to have a skipping rope to play with.

(*MARY takes the skipping rope and throws it down.*)

MARTHA. Mary Lennox.

(*MARY turns back to face her.*)

MARTHA. Tha' forgot tha' rope.

[MUSIC CUE #7B: WHITE HORSE–playoff]

(*MARY grabs the rope and exits.*)

SCENE 2
THE BALLROOM

[MUSIC CUE #8: A GIRL IN THE VALLEY]

ROSE, and other DREAMERS enter dancing a waltz. Something about them seems like a memory. ARCHIBALD stands stage right, as though remembering these scenes. LILY dances alone.

LILY.
A MAN WHO CAME TO MY VALLEY,
A MAN I HARDLY KNEW.
A MAN WHO CAME TO MY GARDEN,

GREW TO LOVE ME.
    ARCHIBALD. (*Begins to move into the scene as he sings.*)
A GIRL I SAW IN A VALLEY,
A GIRL I HARDLY KNEW.
A GIRL AT WORK IN A GARDEN,
GREW TO LOVE ME.

(*ARCHIBALD begins to dance now too, the MUSIC drawing them together.*)

    LILY.
FROM THE GATE, HE
CALLED OUT SO KINDLY,
"LASS WOULDST THOU 'LOW ME
REST HERE, I'VE RIDDEN QUITE FAR."
    ARCHIBALD.
"SHARE MY TEA," SHE
BADE ME SO GENTLY,
OATCAKES AND CREAM,
SWEET PLUMS IN A JAR.
    LILY.
AND EVERY DAY TO MY GARDEN,
THIS MAN, WHO MIGHT HE BE,
CAME BEARING BASKETS OF ROSES,
FOR HE LOVED ME.
    ARCHIBALD.
ALL I OWN, I'D GIVE —
    LILY.
— JUST A GARDEN
    ARCHIBALD.
ALL I WOULD ASK IS NEVER TO —
    LILY.
—NEVER TO LEAVE
    LILY and ARCHIBALD.
SAY YOU'LL HAVE ME
SAFE YOU WILL KEPP ME
WHERE YOU WOULD LEAD ME

THERE
LILY and ARCHIBALD.
THERE I WOULD, THERE I WOULD
THERE I WOULD GO ...

LILY.	**ARCHIBALD.**
A MAN	
WHO CAME TO MY	A GIRL WHO CAME TO
VALLEY	MY VALLEY
A MAN	A
I HARDLY KNEW	GIRL I HARDLY KNEW
A MAN WHO GAVE ME	A GIRL WHO GAVE ME
A GARDEN	A GARDEN
GREW TO LOVE ME	GREW TO LOVE ME

(They waltz. They are so happy, so deeply in love. And suddenly, MARY enters. The MUSIC stops, and LILY and the other dancers disappear.)

MARY. Are you my Uncle Archibald?
ARCHIBALD. Who's that?
MARY. It's Mary Lennox, sir. Are you my Uncle Archibald?
ARCHIBALD. *(Tries to regain his composure.)* Yes, I am. Good morning, child.
MARY. Are you going to be my father now?
ARCHIBALD. I am your guardian. Though I am a poor one for any child. I offer you ...

(MARY pulls the photograph she brought with her from India out of her pocket. LILY enters.)

MARY. Is this my Aunt Lily, in this picture?
ARCHIBALD. *(Looks at it quickly, this is hard for him.)* Yes it is. Where did you get that?
MARY. It was on my dresser, in India. Maybe Mother put it there. I don't know.

(ROSE appears, as though at a ball, and wanders over to talk to LILY.)

ARCHIBALD. Your mother and my Lily ... *(She grabs the photo back from him.)* Please excuse me. *(He notices her coat.)* Who dressed you, child?
MARY. Martha tried to, sir.
ARCHIBALD. Yes, I see. *(He bends over and attempts to button her coat.)*

[MUSIC CUE #8A: LILY AND ROSE]

ROSE. Lily, you've been dancing with that gloomy Archibald all evening!
LILY. He's just shy, Rose. I think Archie has the tenderest heart I've ever known.
ROSE. Silly Lily. Have you been so busy looking into his eyes, that you've missed the hump on his back? *(ROSE laughs and they exit.)*
ARCHIBALD. *(Turning to leave.)* I do hope you'll enjoy the gardens.
MARY. But I want to know what happens to dead people.

(He stops. Death is a subject he cannot resist.)

ARCHIBALD. Yes. Well. Quite natural that you should wonder that. *(A moment.)* We bury them. We put their things away, we remember things they said. We ... talk to them, sometimes ... in our minds, of course ...
MARY. Can they hear us?
ARCHIBALD. *(And now he seems angry at himself.)* And then one morning, when we think we're over them at last, we find ourselves in the ballroom, knowing full well we have been here all night, and we draw the painful conclusion that we have been dancing with them again.
MARY. I don't understand.

ARCHIBALD. Nor will you ever. They're not gone, you see. Just dead.
MARY. Is my Aunt Lily a ghost now?
ARCHIBALD. (*He stops.*) Why, have you heard her?
MARY. I heard *someone* crying in the house last night. But I don't know anything about ghosts. Is my father a ghost now? Does everyone who dies become a ghost?
ARCHIBALD. They're only a ghost if someone alive is still holding onto them.
MARY. Maybe what I heard was Mother, telling me to be nice so you'll keep me.

(*Now, perceiving her fear, he attempts to reassure her.*)

ARCHIBALD. The house *is* haunted, child. Day and night. But it is yours to live in as long as I am master here. I offer you my deepest sympathies on your arrival.

(*Then he walks away. But when he is gone, MARY calls after him.*)

MARY. Did my mother have any *other* family? (*MARY exits.*)

[MUSIC CUE #9: IT'S A MAZE]

SCENE 3
IN THE MAZE

BEN WEATHERSTAFF, the gardener, is at work. MARY is wandering in the gardens.

MARY.
SKIP, SKIPPED THE LADIES TO THE MASTER'S
GATE.
SIP, SIPPED THE LADIES WHILE THE MASTER
ATE.
TIP-TOED THE CHAMBERMAID AND STOLE THEIR
PEARLS.
SNIP, SNIPPED THE GARDENER AND CUT OFF
THEIR CURLS.
MARTHA.
IT'S A MAZE, THIS GARDEN, IT'S A MAZE OF
WAYS
ANY MAN CAN SPEND HIS DAY
IT'S A MAZE, THIS GARDEN, IT'S A MAZE OF
PATHS
BUT A SOUL CAN FIND THE WAY.
BEN.
FOR AN OLD MAN KNOWS HOW A YEAR IT GOES,
HOW THE COLD HARD GROUND IN THE SPRING
COMES ROUND
HOW THE SEEDS TAKE HOLD, AND THE FERNS
UNFOLD
HOW AN ENGLISH GARDEN GROWS.

(MARY is learning to skip rope, and singing.)

MARY.
SKIP, SKIPPED THE LADIES TO THE MASTER'S
GATE.
SIP, SIPPED THE LADIES WHILE THE MASTER
ATE.

DICKON.	BEN.	MARTHA	MARY.
COME			TIP TOED
ALONG,			THE
LOVE			CHAM-
			BERMAID

COME FLY
  AWAY

FLY ALONG

COME
  ALONG
FLY AWAY
  HOME.

COME
  ALONG,
  LOVE
YOU'VE
  COME
A LONG
  WAY
YOU'VE
  FLOWN
ALL THE
  DAY,
COME FLY
  AWAY
    HOME.

TAKE A
  LEFT AND
  THEN
TURNING
  LEFT
  AGAIN
HOW A
  SOUL
  CAN
FIND THE
  WAY

FOR AN OLD
  MAN
  KNOWS,

IT'S A
MAZE THIS
  GARDEN

IT'S A MAZE

OF PATHS

MEANT TO
  LEAD
A MAN

ASTRAY

IT'S A MAZE
  THIS
  GARDEN

AND STOLE
  THEIR
  PEARLS

SNIP,
  SNIPPED
THE GAR-
  DENER
AND CUT
  OFF
  THEIR
  CURLS

DICKON.	BEN.	MARTHA.	MARY.
	HOW A YEAR IT GOES	IT'S A MAZE OF WAYS	
COME FLY AWAY HOME COME FLY	HOW THE COLD HARD GROUND IN THE SPRING COMES ROUND	IT'S A MAZE OF WAYS	
AWAY HOME	HOW IN		
	TIME IT SHOWS HOW A		SKIP, SKIPPED THE LADIES
COME ALONG	GARDEN	TAKE	SIP, SIPPED
LOVE	GROWS,	A LEFT	THE LADIES
COME FLY AWAY	HOW AN ENGLISH	AND THEN	SKIP
FLY AWAY HOME	GARDEN GROWS.	IT'S A MAZE IT'S A MAZE	SIP SKIP

THE GREENHOUSE

MARY.

SKIP, SKIPPED THE LADIES TO THE MASTER'S
   GATE.
SIP, SIPPED THE LADIES WHILE THE MASTER
   ATE.
TIP-TOED THE CHAMBERMAID AND STOLE THEIR
   PEARLS.
SNIP, SNIPPED THE GARDENER AND CUT OFF
   THEIR CURLS.
   (*MARY enters the greenhouse carrying her skipping
rope. Spoken.*) Good morning, Ben.

BEN. Back again today, are you? What have you been doin' out there?

MARY. Just wandering around. I don't have anybody to play with and nothing to do.

BEN. Dickon's here. Why don't you go talk to him? I saw him myself not five minutes ago, conjurin' with that stick of his.

MARY. I haven't met Dickon. I'm not sure he even exists. I think you and Martha just made him up.

BEN. Well, then, I'll give you a spade if you want to dig a little hole somewhere.

MARY. A little hole for what?

BEN. You and me are a good bit alike. We're neither of us good looking, and we're both as sour as we look.

(There is a moment.)

MARY. I saw that robin again today.

BEN. Well, of course you did. There never was his like for bein' meddlesome. He's the real head gardener around here. Chirpin' at me to come see some bush needs prunin'.

MARY. I know where he lives too. It's that walled garden with the tall hedge all around it, and no door, and that funny tree growing out over the top of the wall. I think that tree is the same one my Aunt Lily is sitting in, in this picture.

(MARY pulls the photo out to show him. He is so moved by the picture, he doesn't say anything.)

MARY. Am I right?

BEN. That's the one, missy. That it is. That was Miss Lily's garden.

MARY. Her garden? But I want to see it. Can you show me the door?

BEN. No I can't. When she died, your Uncle Archibald locked the door, said nobody was ever to go in that garden again, and buried the key. And now the ivy's grown up over the door such that I don't even know where it is now.

MARY. But aren't you worried that the garden is all dead with nobody taking care of it?

BEN. Of course I am. But if I so much as set foot in there ...

MARY. Maybe the real reason the robin is chirping at you is he wants you to climb over his garden wall and work on it.

BEN. Maybe he does, but I can't go losin' my job on the advice of a bird, now can I? And the same goes for you.

MARY. My Uncle Archie said ...

BEN. Your Uncle Archie is gone most of the time, missy, and who's to say what might happen if he weren't here to stop it.

(She thinks a moment. [MUSIC CUE # 9A: INDIA STING #2] The FAKIR appears.)

MARY. Do you believe in spirits?

BEN. Old place like this there's more of them than there are of us.

MARY. I heard that crying in the house again last night.

BEN. That could well be a spirit you heard. They like a tall ceiling and a long hallway to swoop around in.

MARY. In India, once, [MUSIC CUE # 9B: BIG DEAD SNAKE] I saw a spirit pull a big dead snake right up out of a basket and make him dance.

BEN. I'm sure you think you've seen just about everything, Missy, except the inside of that garden ... and you keep it that way. You hear me?

(MARY hears the sound of the ROBIN.)

MARY. Good day, Ben. [MUSIC CUE #10: WINTER'S ON THE WING] (*MARY leaves the greenhouse, led by the sound of the ROBIN.*)

THE EDGE OF THE MOOR

(*DICKON is revealed in another part of the garden. He looks above him, as though he has just released a wild bird into the sky.*)

DICKON. (*Sings.*)
WINTER'S ON THE WING,
HERE'S A FINE SPRING MORN,
COMIN' CLEAN THROUGH THE NIGHT,
COME THE MAY ... I SAY
WINTER'S TAKIN' FLIGHT,
SWEEPIN' DARK COLD AIR
OUT TO SEA, SPRING IS BORN,
COMES THE DAY ... I SAY

AND YOU'LL BE HERE TO SEE IT.
STAND AND BREATHE IT ALL THE DAY.
STOOP AND FEEL IT, STOP AND HEAR IT,
SPRING, I SAY.

I SAY
BE GONE, YE HOWLING GALES, BE OFF YE
FROSTY MORNS.
ALL YE SOLID STREAMS BEGIN TO THAW.
MELT, YE WATERFALLS, PART YE FROZEN
WINTERWALLS,
SEE ... SEE NOW IT'S STARTING ...

AND YOU'LL BE HERE TO SEE IT.
STAND AND BREATHE IT ALL THE DAY.
STOOP AND FEEL IT, STOP AND HEAR IT,
SPRING, I SAY.

AND NOW THE SUN IS CLIMBIN' HIGH,
RISING FAST, ON FIRE,
GLARING DOWN THROUGH THE GLOOM,
GONE THE GRAY, I SAY
THE SUN SPELLS THE DOOM
OF THE WINTER'S REIGN.
ICE AND CHILL MUST RETIRE,
COMES THE MAY, SAY I.

    AND YOU'LL BE HERE TO SEE IT.
    STAND AND BREATHE IT ALL THE DAY.
    STOOP AND FEEL IT, STOP AND HEAR IT.
    SPRING, I SAY.

AND NOW THE MIST IS LIFTIN' HIGH
LEAVIN' BRIGHT BLUE AIR,
ROLLIN' CLEAR 'CROSS THE MOOR,
COMES THE MAY, I SAY,
THE STORM'LL SOON BE BY
LEAVIN' CLEAR BLUE SKY.
SOON THE SUN WILL SHINE.
COMES THE DAY, SAY I

    AND YOU'LL BE HERE TO SEE IT.
    STAND AND BREATHE IT ALL THE DAY.
    STOP AND FEEL IT, STOP AND HEAR IT,
    SPRING, I SAY.

        [MUSIC CUE #10A: MARY'S MAZE]

(MARY enters, skipping rather proficiently now, and singing a section of "It's a Maze" on "la." DICKON appears from behind a topiary.)

DICKON. Hello there, Mary.
MARY. Who are you?
DICKON. I'm Martha's brother, Dickon. I hope I didn't fright thee.

MARY. But what are you doing here?
DICKON. I did fright thee. I'm sorry.
MARY. But why haven't I seen you before?
DICKON. A body has to move gentle and speak low when wild things is about.
MARY. You mean you're here all the time?
DICKON. Well, if somethin' is sick I take a look at it, sure I do. And find the ponies that wander off and the eggs that roll out of the nests, but look here. Me mother's sent you a penny's worth of seeds for your garden.

[MUSIC CUE # 10B: ROBIN CUES]

(A ROBIN whistle is heard.)

DICKON. There's columbine and poppies by the handful.
MARY. I don't have a garden.
DICKON. But don't you want one? One of your own, I mean.

(MARY isn't sure she wants to talk to him, but his spell is beginning to work on her.)

DICKON. Come and look at your seeds, why don't you? Well, if you don't want 'em, I'll ...

(She approaches quickly now, and he pours the seeds in her hand.
The ROBIN is heard again.)

MARY. I want to go in that garden. Where the robin lives.
DICKON. I wasn't sure you'd seen him.
MARY. Seen him? He's done nothing but chirp at me ever since I got here.

(The ROBIN whistles.)

DICKON. Well, you have to understand, he's makin' his nest. And he can't afford to have you interferin' if you're not friendly.

(The ROBIN whistles again. DICKON takes Mary's skipping rope and begins to play with it.)

MARY. How do you know that?

DICKON. Because we were just talkin' about you, how do you think?

MARY. He was talking too, or just you?

DICKON. What he thinks, is that you're lookin' for a nest yourself, only it looks to him like your nest would have to be pretty big.

MARY. Have you ever been in there?

DICKON. It's not mine to go into, Mary. But it might be yours, I can't say. He's been keepin' it safe for somebody, that much I know.

MARY. He has?

DICKON. Same way as the ivy grown up to hide the door. But maybe the robin is waitin' to hear why you want to go in there, exactly. Bein' as he's got the safest nestin' spot in all England, he's wise to be wary.

MARY. Can you tell him I'm friendly?

DICKON. I could, but what if you wanted to tell him something else and I wasn't here. Be much quicker if you learned to talk to him yourself.

MARY. But what could I say that he would understand?

DICKON. Well I wouldn't mention you were an egg-eater, if you know what I mean. But are you interested in flyin' perhaps? Or bugs?

MARY. I'm afraid not.

DICKON. Well, then just tell him about yourself, and I'll translate into Yorkshire for you 'til you get the way of it.

[MUSIC CUE #11: SHOW ME THE KEY]

(The ROBIN trills.)

MARY.
I ...
DICKON.
SHE ...
MARY.
I'M A GIRL ...
DICKON.
SHE IS A LASS,
AS TOOK A GRAIDLEY FANCY TO THEE.
DOST THA' FEAR?
MARY.
THA' MUN NOT FEAR.
DICKON.
SHE'S TOOK THEE ON
FOR LIKE TO VEX THEE.
NOWT O' THE SOART.
MARY.
NOWT O' THE SOART.
DICKON.
SHE KNOWS FAIR WELL
SHE MUN NOT FRIGHT THEE.
MARY
CANNA THA' SHOW ME ...
DICKON.
FAIR BETTER TO KNOW HER ...
MARY.
SHOW ME THA' KEY.
DICKON.
SHOW HER THA' KEY.

(The ROBIN trills again.)

DICKON.
SHE'S A LASS AND THA ART' RIGHT,

AS NEEDS A SPOT WHERE SHE CAN REST IN.
MARY.
I MUN SIT, WHERE I'LL NOT BE
SO THINKIN' THOUGHTS OR FEEL A GUEST IN.
DICKON.
NOWT O' THE SOART.
MARY.
NOWT O' THE SOART.
DICKON.
SHE'D FAIR BE WATCHIN' FOR THE SPRING.
MARY.
I'LL NOT BE CLIMBIN UP, I'LL ONLY BE CALLIN'
GOOD MORNING, AND FAIR LOW I'LL SING.
DICKON. Well done, Mary.

(The ROBIN trills again, and
LILY and ROSE wander into the maze.)

ROSE. Lily, what are you looking for?
LILY. Wait 'til you see it. It's the most beautiful
garden I ever ... and nobody knows about it except
Archie, but the door is so covered over with ivy that I can
never find it. Oh, wait, maybe it's on this other side.
MARY.
I'LL ONLY WALK AROUND AS LIKE TO SEE IT
    FOR MYSEL'.
IF THA' CANST 'LOW ME VISIT I'LL SPEAK LOW
    E'EN TO THYSEL'.
THA'LL NOT BE POTHERED NIGHT AND DAY BY
    WENCHES RACIN' ROUND.
I'LL BUT SEEM A SILENT DREAM, STANDIN' ON
    THE SECRET GROUND.

I'D BUT SMELL THE GROWIN' THINGS, COUNT
    THE ROSES 'GAINST THE WALL.
HEAR THY BABES WHEN FIRST THEY PECK,
    STRETCH MY HAND IF THEY SHOULD FALL.

OR IF THA' LIKES, I'LL BRING THEE SEEDS OR
WORMS ALL IN A MOUND.
FOR IF THA'LL HAVE ME FOR A FRIEND ...
THA'LL BE THE FIRST I'VE FOUND.
MARY.
I'M A LASS.
DICKON.
A TRUSTY LASS.
MARY.
THAT TOOK A GRAIDLEY FANCY TO THEE.
CANNA THA' SHOW ME —
DICKON.
FAIR WELL DOST THA' KNOW HER ...
MARY.
SHOW ME THA' KEY.
MARY and DICKON.
SHOW ME (HER) THA' KEY.
DICKON. Well, then. I'm off, then.
MARY. But where are you going?
DICKON. I can't say. But I'll see you tomorrow
sure enough. And if you need me before then, well, now
that you and robin is talking, he always knows where I
am.
MARY. But can't you help me look for the key?
DICKON. But that's why I'm leavin', Mary. A body
can't find a thing in a crowd.
MARY. All right, then. Bye.
DICKON. (*Stands behind her and sings.*)
AND YOU'LL BE HERE TO SEE IT.
STAND AND BREATHE IT ALL THE DAY.
STOOP AND FEEL IT, STOP AND HEAR IT,
SPRING ... I SAY.

(*DICKON hangs the skipping rope around one of the
topiaries and exits.*)

MARTHA. (*Calling from offstage.*) Mary Lennox!

(MARY starts to leave, but the ROBIN stops her with a trill, reminding her, perhaps, to take her skipping rope. MARY pulls the rope off the topiary and hears a metallic CLINK.)

MARY. Oh, no. Look what I've ...

(Something has fallen into the leaves at her feet.)

MARY. What was that? *(She bends over to pick it up, brushing away the leaves where it is now buried.)* Where did it ... *(She searches for it.)* There it is! *(She picks it up.)* It's a key! It's the key to the garden! I found the key to the garden! It was right here! *(She looks up at the robin.)* But the door! Where is the door? *(She hears MARTHA calling her.)*

MARTHA. *(From offstage.)* Mary Lennox!

MARY. *(Puts the key in her pocket quickly and runs toward the house.)* Coming!

MARTHA. *(Enters, looking for MARY.)* Mary Lennox! We haven't got time to play hide and seek now. Mrs. Medlock wants us in the house right now! [MUSIC CUE #11A: SKIP, SKIPPED–TRANSITION] Mary! *(MARTHA exits, looking for MARY.)*

AYAH and FAKIR.
SKIP, SKIPPED THE LADIES TO THE MASTER'S
      GATE.
SIP, SIPPED THE LADIES WHILE THE MASTER
      ATE.
TIP-TOED THE CHAMBERMAID AND STOLE THEIR
      PEARLS.
SNIP, SNIPPED THE GARDENER AND CUT OFF
      THEIR CURLS.

SCENE 4
ARCHIBALD'S LIBRARY

DR. CRAVEN is seated at the desk, as ARCHIBALD enters, wearing a heavy raincoat.

ARCHIBALD. Will this rain never stop?
DR. CRAVEN. Archie, I'm so pleased. I've finally located a suitable school for young Mary.
ARCHIBALD. A school?
DR. CRAVEN. She needs the company of other children. Particularly after a tragedy such as this.
ARCHIBALD. But she's practically just arrived, Neville. Does she want to leave?
DR. CRAVEN. This is no house for a child. What will she have to do here? Wander the halls?
ARCHIBALD. As I do, you mean? What a wretched house this is. Father should have given Misselthwaite to you, Neville, not me.
DR. CRAVEN. You are the elder brother, Archie. That would never have occurred to him. But if you continue to feel you cannot live here, then leave. You were happy once before. In Paris. You're still a young man. There is no reason ...
ARCHIBALD. I can't leave, Neville.
DR. CRAVEN. But what good does it do to sit by the boy's bed, night after night, hoping for a miracle?
ARCHIBALD. They have been known to happen.
DR. CRAVEN. When Lily died, I gave up my practice to care for the ...
ARCHIBALD. You've been completely faithful, Neville. I am deeply grateful.
DR. CRAVEN. But I did not give up my responsibility to *you,* Archie. I cannot allow you to waste your life waiting for the inevitable end. I cannot.
ARCHIBALD. I am not wasting my life, Neville. This *is* my life now.

(MRS. MEDLOCK enters, with MARY.)

MRS. MEDLOCK. Beg pardon, sir, you sent for young Mary.
ARCHIBALD. Yes, child. Come in. Perhaps we can manage to have a moment before the storm carries us away. Take a chair.
MARY. *(Takes a seat.)* Thank you, sir.

(And then ARCHIBALD realizes he has no idea what he intended to say to MARY.)

ARCHIBALD. Are you well? Do they take good care of you?
MARY. Yes, sir. Thank you, sir.
ARCHIBALD. I'm sorry it's been so long since we've spoken. It's just I keep forgetting you. *(Another pause.)* I intended to find you a school to go to or ...
MARY. Oh no, Please don't send me away!
ARCHIBALD. No, of course not. But perhaps you would enjoy a governess, considering that you've had a chance to look around now and know there's nothing for you to do. What do you say to that?
MARY. Please don't make me have a governess, sir. There's everything for me to do here. There are so many gardens to walk around in, and so much to learn about them. Martha gave me a skipping rope, and Dickon gave me some seeds and ...

(ALBERT appears upstage IN THE PAST.)

ALBERT. And here's a rose for you, Mary ...
ARCHIBALD. Yes, all right then ...
ALBERT. Happy birthday, darling.

(LILY enters.)

ARCHIBALD. Play outside if you like, but is there anything you need? Would you like some toys, or books or dolls perhaps?
MARY. Might I ...
ARCHIBALD. Speak up, child.
MARY. Might I have a bit of earth, sir?
ARCHIBALD. A bit of earth?
MARY. To plant seeds in, yes sir. A garden.

(ARCHIBALD is clearly moved by this request. This is exactly the way Lily used to talk. NEVILLE is alarmed.)

ARCHIBALD. Do you care about gardens so much, then?
MARY. I didn't know about them in India. I was always ill and tired and it was too hot. I sometimes played at making little flower beds, sticking things in the sand. But here, I might have a real garden if you would allow it, sir.
ARCHIBALD. Are you sure there's nothing else?
MARY. No, sir.
ARCHIBALD. All right, then. You may have your earth. Take as much earth as you want.
MARY. Thank you very much, sir.

(He tries to indicate that MARY may leave the room. But she mistakes his gesture for a wave, and waves back.)

DR. CRAVEN. You may leave child.

(MARY leaves the room, and after a moment, ARCHIBALD turns to DR. CRAVEN.)

ARCHIBALD. It's much worse being back this time. The dreams are much more vivid. And I hear things. In the halls.
DR. CRAVEN. It's the girl, Archie.

ARCHIBALD. Do you mean Mary? But I never see
her.

DR. CRAVEN. Because you can't see her, Archie,
because she reminds you of Lily.

ARCHIBALD. You can't be serious.

DR. CRAVEN. I can see the resemblance, myself.
Although Lily's hair was more ...You were very kind to
take the girl in, Archie, but in your state, it's simply too
much. If you allow the girl to stay here, to grow up here,
I have no doubt your dreams, to say the very least, will
get even worse.

ARCHIBALD. But you can see the girl is lonely,
Neville. Perhaps I should have *more* conversations with
her.

DR. CRAVEN. I don't think that is wise, Archie.

[MUSIC CUE #12: A BIT OF EARTH]

ARCHIBALD. A bit of earth ...

DR. CRAVEN. Until you are ready to send her to a
school ...

ARCHIBALD.	**DR. CRAVEN.**
SHE WANTS A LITTLE	It is my professional advice
BIT OF EARTH.	that you continue to obey your
SHE'LL PLANT SOME SEEDS.	natural instincts and avoid her.

ARCHIBALD.
THE SEEDS WILL GROW.

DR. CRAVEN. Archie ...

ARCHIBALD.
THE FLOWERS BLOOM.
BUT IS THEIR BOUNTY
WHAT SHE NEEDS ....

DR. CRAVEN. If I could have your signature on
these leases.

ARCHIBALD.
HOW CAN SHE CHANCE   (*DR CRAVEN exits.*)
TO LOVE A LITTLE
BIT OF EARTH?
DOES SHE NOT KNOW?
THE EARTH IS OLD,
AND DOESN'T CARE IF
ONE SMALL GIRL WANTS THINGS
TO GROW.

SHE NEEDS A FRIEND.
SHE NEEDS A FATHER,
BROTHER, SISTER,
MOTHER'S ARMS.
SHE NEEDS TO LAUGH,
SHE NEEDS TO DANCE
AND LEARN TO WORK
HER GIRLISH CHARMS.

SHE NEEDS A HOME.
THE ONLY THING
SHE REALLY NEEDS
I CANNOT GIVE.
INSTEAD SHE ASKS,
A BIT OF EARTH,
TO MAKE IT LIVE.

SHE SHOULD HAVE A PONY.
GALLOP CROSS THE MOOR.
SHE SHOULD HAVE A DOLL'S HOUSE,
WITH A HUNDRED ROOMS PER FLOOR.
WHY CAN'T SHE ASK FOR A TREASURE?
SOMETHING THAT MONEY CAN BUY,
THAT WON'T DIE. WHEN
I'D GIVE HER THE WORLD,
SHE ASKS, INSTEAD ...
FOR SOME EARTH.

A BIT OF EARTH
SHE WANTS A LITTLE
BIT OF EARTH.
SHE'LL PLANT SOME SEEDS.
THE SEEDS WILL GROW.
THE FLOWERS
BLOOM, THEIR BEAUTY
JUST THE THING SHE NEEDS ...

SHE'LL GROW TO LOVE THE TENDER ROSES,
LILIES FAIR,
THE IRIS TALL.
AND THEN IN FALL,
HER BIT OF EARTH
WILL FREEZE AND KILL THEM ALL,
A BIT OF EARTH, A BIT OF EARTH,

(And with a crash of THUNDER and a stroke of LIGHTNING, the storm hits.)

SCENE 5
MISSELTHWAITE MANOR
IN THE GALLERY

[MUSIC CUE #13: STORM I]

LARGE PORTRAITS of LILY loom in the air, as the DREAMERS circle around ARCHIBALD, and sing.

MAJOR HOLMES.
CLOSE THE SHUTTERS AND LOCK THE DOORS.
ALBERT.
BRACE THE WINDOWS AS IN IT POURS.
FAKIR.
CANDLES ONLY THE ONES YOU CARRY,

LIEUTENANT SHAW.
WATCH NOW —
LIEUTENANT WRIGHT.
CAREFUL THE STAIRS,
WRIGHT AND SHAW.
WORKING IN PAIRS,
ALBERT.
FARES WELL THE HOUSE THAT'S READY ...
DREAMERS.
COMIN' A TERRIBLE STORM.
LOOKS LIKE THE SEA IN A GALE.
BRANCHES ARE BROKEN IN HALF.
CARRIED ALOFT LIKE A SAIL.
NOT SINCE I WAS A CHILD, HAVE I
HEARD SUCH A HORRIBLE WAIL.

AH ...

(There is a LULL in the storm, and DR. CRAVEN stands thinking about the other storm he knows is brewing.)

[MUSIC CUE #14: LILY'S EYES]

DR. CRAVEN.
STRANGELY QUIET, BUT NOW THE STORM
SIMPLY RESTS TO STRIKE AGAIN.
STANDING, WAITING, I THINK OF HER,
I THINK OF HER ...

(ARCHIBALD, is also looking at a portrait of Lily.)

ARCHIBALD.
STRANGE, THIS MARY, SHE LEAVES THE ROOM,
YET REMAINS, SHE LINGERS ON.
SOMETHING STIRS ME TO THINK OF HER,
I THINK OF HER ...
DR. CRAVEN.
FROM DEATH SHE CASTS HER SPELL.

ALL NIGHT WE HEAR HER SIGHS.
AND NOW A GIRL HAS COME
WHO HAS HER EYES.

SHE HAS HER EYES, THE GIRL HAS LILY'S
    HAZEL EYES.
THOSE EYES THAT SAW HIM HAPPY LONG AGO.
THOSE EYES THAT GAVE HIM LIFE AND HOPE
    HE'D NEVER KNOWN.
HOW CAN HE SEE THE GIRL AND MISS THOSE
    HAZEL EYES.
    ARCHIBALD.
SHE HAS HER EYES, THE GIRL HAS LILY'S
    HAZEL EYES.
THOSE EYES THAT CLOSED AND LEFT ME ALL
    ALONE.
THOSE EYES I FEEL WILL NEVER EVER LET ME
    GO,
HOW CAN I SEE THIS GIRL WHO HAS HER HAZEL
    EYES.

IN LILY'S EYES, A CASTLE
THIS HOUSE SEEMED TO BE.
AND I HER BRAVEST KNIGHT BECAME,
MY LADY FAIR WAS SHE.
    DR. CRAVEN. (*Angry and hurt.*)
SHE HAS HER EYES, SHE HAS MY LILY'S HAZEL
    EYES.
THOSE EYES THAT LOVED MY BROTHER, NEVER
    ME.
THOSE EYES THAT NEVER SAW ME, NEVER
    KNEW I LONGED
TO HOLD HER CLOSE, TO LIVE AT LAST IN LILY'S
    EYES.
    ARCHIBALD.
IMAGINE ME, A LOVER ...
    DR. CRAVEN.
I LONGED FOR THE DAY

SHE'D TURN AND SEE ME STANDING THERE —
ARCHIBALD and CRAVEN.
WOULD GOD HAD LET HER STAY.

DR. CRAVEN.	**ARCHIBALD.**
SHE HAS HER EYES,	SHE HAS HER EYES,
SHE HAS LILY'S	MY LILY'S HAZEL
HAZEL EYES.	EYES
	THOSE EYES THAT
	SAW ME
THOSE EYES THAT	HAPPY LONG AGO.
FIRST I LOVED SO	
HOW CAN	HOW CAN
I NOW FORGET	I NOW FORGET
THAT I DARED TO BE	THAT ONCE I DARED
	TO BE ...
IN LOVE,	IN LOVE,
ALIVE, AND WHOLE	ALIVE AND WHOLE
IN LILY'S EYES.	IN LILY'S EYES.
IN LILY'S EYES...	IN LILY'S EYES...

SCENE 6
THE HALLWAY

[MUSIC CUE #15: STORM II]

MARY enters the gallery, holding a candle. MARTHA,
LILY and the DREAMERS also wander the gallery.

MARY.
SOMEONE IS CRYING, JUST NOW I HEARD
    THEM.
SOMEONE IN THIS HOUSE IS CRYING.
WHY WON'T THEY TELL ME, I KNOW THEY'RE
    LYING?
SOMEONE HERE IS LOST OR MAD.
I MUST TRY TO FIND THEM,
BEG THEM STOP SO I CAN SLEEP.

I HEARD SOMEONE CRYING.
WHO THO' COULD IT BE?
SOMEONE IN THIS HOUSE,
WHOM NO ONE SEES TO SEE.
SOMEONE NO ONE SEEMS TO
HEAR EXCEPT FOR ME ...
I HEARD SOMEONE CRYING ...
   MARY and AYAH.
I HEARD SOMEONE CRYING ...
   DREAMERS.
AH...........................
....
....

(MARY walks through the halls. There is a terrible THUNDERCLAP, and the DREAMERS lead MARY to a room she hasn't seen before.)

SCENE 7
COLIN'S ROOM

A GHOSTLY FORM lies on a bed, screaming. MARY is terrified.

COLIN. Get out!
MARY. Who are *you*?
COLIN. Who are *you*? Are you a ghost?
MARY. No I am not. I am Mary Lennox. Archibald Craven is my uncle.
COLIN. How do I know you're not a ghost?
MARY. I'll pinch you if you like. That will show you how real I am. Who are *you*?
COLIN. I am Colin. Mr. Craven is my *father*. I see no one and no one sees me. Including my father. I am going to die.
MARY. How do you know?

COLIN. Because I hear everybody whispering about it. If I live, I may be a hunchback, but I shan't live.

MARY. Well, I've seen lots of dead people, and you don't look like any of *them*.

COLIN. Dead people! Where did you *come* from?

MARY. From India. My parents died there of the cholera. But I don't know what happened to them after that. Perhaps they burned them, I don't know.

COLIN. My mother died when I was born. That's why my father hates me.

MARY. He hates the garden too.

COLIN. What garden?

MARY. (*Wishes she hadn't said anything about the garden.*) Just a garden your mother liked. Have you always been in this bed?

COLIN. Sometimes I have been taken to places at the seaside, but I won't stay because people stare at me. And one time a grand doctor came from London, and said to take off this iron thing Dr. Craven made me wear, and keep me out in the fresh air. But I hate fresh air, and I won't be taken out.

MARY. If you don't like people to see you, do you want me to go away?

COLIN. Yes, but I want you to come back first thing tomorrow morning and tell me all about India. In the books my father sends me, I've read that elephants can swim. Have you ever seen them swim? They seem altogether too large to be swimmers, unless maybe they use their ears to ...

MARY. I can't come talk to you in the morning. I have to go outside and look for something with Dickon.

COLIN. Who's Dickon?

MARY. He's Martha's brother. He's my friend.

(Suddenly, COLIN's despotic temperament flares.)

COLIN. If you go outside with that Dickon instead of coming here to talk to me, I'll send him away.

MARY. You *can't* send Dickon away!

COLIN. I can do whatever I want. If I were to live, this entire place would belong to me someday. And they *all* know that.

MARY. You little Rajah! If you send Dickon away, I'll never come into this room again.

COLIN. I'll make you. They'll drag you in here.

MARY. I won't even look at you. I'll stare at the floor.

COLIN. You are a selfish thing.

MARY. You're more selfish than I am. You're the most selfish boy I ever saw.

COLIN. I'm selfish because I'm dying.

MARY. You just say that to make people feel sorry for you. If you were a nice boy it might be true, but you're too nasty to die!

(MARY turns and stomps away toward the door. [MUSIC CUE #15A: INDIA STING #3] The AYAH appears.)

COLIN. No, please don't go.

(She stops.)

COLIN. It's just that the storm scares me so that if I went to sleep, I'm afraid I might not wake up.

[MUSIC CUE #16: ROUND-SHOULDERED MAN]

MARY. Then close your eyes, and I will do what my Ayah used to do in India. I will pat your hand and stroke it and sing something quite low.

(The AYAH begins to hum.)

COLIN. And I have such terrible dreams.

MARY. I have bad dreams too. Last night I dreamed about my father. Only he had this lump on his back, like your father. And then, when he turned around, he *was* your father.

COLIN.
SOME NIGHTS I DREAM
THAT A ROUND-SHOULDERED MAN
COMES IN MY ROOM
ON A BEAM OF MOONLIGHT.
HE NEVER SAYS WHAT HE WANTS,
HE JUST SITS WITH A BOOK IN HIS HANDS.

AND THEN I DREAM
THAT THE ROUND-SHOULDERED MAN
TAKES ME OFF ON A RIDE
THROUGH THE MOORS BY MOONLIGHT.
HE NEVER SAYS, WHERE WE'LL GO
WE JUST RIDE 'CROSS THE HILLS TILL DAWN.

AND SOME NIGHT I'M GOING TO ASK HIM,
IS THE NIGHT SKY BLACK OR BLUE?
I KNOW THE ANSWER'S IN HIS BOOK
OF ALL THAT'S GOOD AND TRUE.

MARY. It's no wonder you have bad dreams. The shadows in this room are so strange.

COLIN.
AND ONCE I DREAMED
THAT THE ROUND-SHOULDERED MAN
TOOK MY HAND AND WE WALKED
TO A SECRET GARDEN.
I HEARD MY FATHER SPEAK MY NAME
AS WE SAT IN THE CROOK OF A BROKEN TREE.

COLIN.	**MARY.**
AND SOME NIGHT I'M GOING TO ASK HIM	AND SOME NIGHT I THINK YOU SHOULD ASK HIM

COLIN and MARY.
HOW THE OLD MOON TURNS TO NEW
  COLIN.
I KNOW THE ANSWER'S IN HIS BOOK
OF ALL THAT'S GOOD AND TRUE
  COLIN and MARY.
I'M SURE THE ANSWER'S IN HIS BOOK
OF ALL THAT'S GOOD AND TRUE.
  MARY. Colin, I just realized ...We're cousins.

*(Suddenly, MEDLOCK and DR. CRAVEN enter.
CRAVEN goes to the boy. MEDLOCK grabs MARY.)*

  MRS. MEDLOCK. Mary Lennox!

(MRS. MEDLOCK pulls MARY away from the bed.)

  CRAVEN. (*Preparing an injection.*) I was afraid of
something like this.
  COLIN. No! No! I don't want an ...
  DR. CRAVEN. He must have his rest. If she's
been...
  MARY. But I've never seen him before!
  CRAVEN. ... how can I hope to succeed with him if
my orders are not followed.
  MRS. MEDLOCK. I've told her to stay in her
room, but she refuses to obey.
  COLIN. Get away from me! Don't touch me! No!

(ROSE appears.)

  ROSE. Albert!
  MARY. I only wanted him to stop crying.

*(As DR. CRAVEN wrestles with COLIN, MRS.
MEDLOCK takes MARY firmly in hand and walks her
to the door.
ALBERT appears.)*

ROSE. What is that infernal wailing?

[MUSIC CUE #16A: BEFORE FINAL STORM]

ALBERT. It's the servants, Rose.
MRS. MEDLOCK. Now, you listen to me, Mary Lennox.
ALBERT. The cholera. It's quite bad.
MAJOR HOLMES. Ten thousand dead at last count.
MRS. MEDLOCK. Do you see what you've done?
ALBERT. I should have sent you away while there was still time.
MRS. MEDLOCK. You are *never* to see Colin again.
MARY. But why?

(And now other DREAMERS appear, as MARY begins to remember exactly what happened at that dinner party.)

CLAIRE. It's exactly what they deserve. Letting their sewage run in the streets.
MRS. MEDLOCK. The one rule you were given here you have violated.
LIEUTENANT WRIGHT. But how are we to get around with all the dead in frigging flames?
COLIN. No!

(DR. CRAVEN gives COLIN a shot.)

ALICE. They're servants, darling. There are millions of them.
MRS. MEDLOCK. Do you want to speak to her, doctor?
DR. CRAVEN. No!

LIEUTENANT SHAW. I wonder if I might have a glass of water.

(COLIN collapses back on the bed.)

MARY. But why didn't you tell me he was here?
ROSE. I'm very warm, Albert.
MRS. MEDLOCK. Because I was ordered not to. And I obey my orders because I want to keep my place here and I advise you to do the same.
ALBERT. Mary! Where is Mary?
MRS. MEDLOCK. Do you understand?
ALBERT. Someone. Find her. [MUSIC CUE #17: FINAL STORM] There's a child ...

(There is another violent stroke of LIGHTNING and MARY runs out of the room and down the hall in absolute terror.)

SCENE 8
THE MAZE

MARY rushes outside and into the maze.

DREAMERS.
COMIN' A TERRIBLE STORM.
SHAKIN' THE SOULS OF THE DEAD.
QUAKIN' THE FLOOR UNDERFOOT,
SHAKIN' THE ROOF OVER HEAD.
NOT SINCE I WAS A CHILD, HAVE I
FEARED ...

(There is a crash of THUNDER, and the DREAMERS appear, distressed and confused. Finally, MARY remembers what really happened the night her parents died. She approaches each one of them, but as they

dab their faces with the red handkerchiefs, she knows they cannot help her.)

ROSE.
MISTRESS MARY. QUITE CONTRARY,
HOW DOES YOUR GARDEN GROW?
AYAH.
NOT SO WELL, SHE SAID, SEE THE LILY'S DEAD.
DIG IT UP, YOU'RE OUT, YOU GO.
MAJOR HOLMES.
MISTRESS MARY, QUITE CONTRARY,
HOW DOES YOUR GARDEN GROW?
LIEUTENANT SHAW.
FAR TOO HOT, SHE CRIED, SEE MY ROSE HAS DIED.
DIG IT UP AND OUT YOU GO.

(MARY runs wildly, trying to find anyone, anything. But the faster she runs, the more terrified she becomes. The DREAMERS cannot see her now, she is desperately alone.)

ALICE.
MISTRESS MARY, QUITE CONTRARY,
HOW DOES YOUR GARDEN GROW?

CLAIRE.	**DREAMERS.**
OH IT'S DRY, SHE WAILED, SEE THE IRIS FAILED	IT'S A MAZE THIS GARDEN IT'S A MAZE OF WAYS...
DIG IT UP AND OUT YOU GO	
FAKIR.	**DREAMERS.**
MISTRESS MARY, QUITE CONTRARY, HOW DOES YOUR GARDEN	SOMETHING WRONG INSIDE IT. IT'S A MAZE THIS GARDEN,

GROW?

WRIGHT.
HAD AN EARLY
  FROST,

NOW IT'S GONE IT'S
  LOST,
DIG IT UP AND OUT
YOU GO ...

IT'S A MAZE OF
  WAYS...
**WOMEN
DREAMERS.**
HIGH ON A HILL ...

SOMETHING WRONG
  INSIDE IT ...

DREAMERS. *(In a round.)*
IT'S A MAZE THIS GARDEN,
IT'S A MAZE OF WAYS,
MEANT TO LEAD A SOUL ASTRAY.

IT'S A MAZE THIS GARDEN,
IT'S A MAZE OF WAYS,

IT'S A MAZE THIS GARDEN,
IT'S A MAZE OF WAYS,
MEANT TO LEAD A SOUL ASTRAY.

(THE DREAMERS form a circle as in the opening dream. MARY runs round and round it, looking for a way in.)

CLAIRE.	ALICE.	AYAH.	ROSE.
MISTRESS MARY	NOT SINCE I WAS A CHILD	MAH...	CRYING...
MISTRESS MARY	HAVE I FEARED		
MISTRESS MARY	HAVE I FEARED	MISTRESS MARY	SOMEONE CRYING
MISTRESS MARY		MISTRESS MARY	

FAKIR.	ALBERT.	SHAW.
JA...	FOR HER MOTHER	MISTRESS MARY
DU...	THERE'S A GIRL	MISTRESS MARY

| KE... | WHO NO ONE | MISTRESS MARY |
| | SEES...NO ONE | MISTRESS MARY |

WRIGHT.   **HOLMES.**
SKIPPED THE LADIES   WATCH NOW ...
TO THE MASTER'S   WATCH NOW ...
  GATE
SKIPPED THE LADIES   WATCH NOW ...
TO THE MASTER'S
  GATE
DREAMERS.   (ALBERT.)
MISTRESS MARY
  QUITE CONTRARY
HOW DOES YOUR
  GARDEN GROW
HAD AN EARLY FROST
NOW IT'S GONE, IT'S
  LOST
DIG IT UP, AND OUT   (Mary ...!)
  YOU GO
YOU'RE OUT, YOU GO,   (Mary...!)
OUT, YOU GO!

*(MARY looks up and sees her father, the last person alive
to think of her. He kneels, opening his arms and heart
to her, and
She runs into his arms.
And the other DREAMERS disappear from the stage.
As MIST fills the stage, LILY appears.
ALBERT smiles, shows MARY that LILY is waiting for
her, and indicates to MARY that she should go with
LILY now.
Never looking back, MARY walks toward LILY'S open
arms. LILY steps aside, showing MARY the door in
the wall behind her. The door to the Secret Garden.
MARY wipes her eyes, takes out the key, puts it into the
lock, and starts to open the door.)*

END OF ACT I

ACT II

SCENE 1
THE OTHER SIDE OF THE DOOR
THE TEA PARTY DREAM

[MUSIC CUE #19: THE GIRL I MEAN TO BE]

A large tea party celebrating Mary's birthday is in progress. Everyone is there, ARCHIBALD, LILY, ROSE, ALBERT, DICKON, MARTHA, and the DREAMERS, the living and the dead, exactly as MARY would like to see them. A PHOTOGRAPHER stages pictures, a cake is presented, and EVERYONE is serenely happy.

MARY.
I NEED A PLACE WHERE I CAN GO,
WHERE I CAN WHISPER WHAT I KNOW,
WHERE I CAN WHISPER WHO I LIKE,
AND WHERE I GO TO SEE THEM.

I NEED A PLACE WHERE I CAN HIDE,
WHERE NO ONE SEES MY LIFE INSIDE,
WHERE I CAN MAKE MY PLANS AND WRITE
  THEM DOWN
SO I CAN READ THEM.

A PLACE WHERE I CAN BID MY HEART
BE STILL, AND IT WILL MIND ME.
A PLACE WHERE I CAN GO WHEN I AM LOST,
AND THERE I'LL FIND ME.

63

I NEED A PLACE TO SPEND THE DAY,
WHERE NO ONE SAYS TO GO OR STAY,
WHERE I CAN TAKE MY PEN AND DRAW
THE GIRL I MEAN TO BE.

(Suddenly, from nowhere, COLIN is rolled downstage in his wheelchair by MRS. MEDLOCK. DR. CRAVEN, drops a red handkerchief in his lap. [MUSIC CUE #19A: HOUSE ON THE HILL–Transition] The mood turns dark and the DREAMERS sing.)

LIEUTENANTS WRIGHT and SHAW.
HIGH ON A HILL SITS A BIG OLD HOUSE
WITH SOMETHING WRONG INSIDE IT.
SPIRITS HAUNT THE HALLS
AND MAKE NO EFFORT NOW TO HIDE IT.

AND THE MASTER HEARS THE WHISPERS
ON THE STAIRWAYS DARK AND STILL.
AND THE SPIRITS SPEAK OF SECRETS
IN THE HOUSE UPON THE HILL.

SCENE TWO
ARCHIBALD'S DRESSING ROOM

DR. CRAVEN comes into ARCHIBALD'S dressing room. ARCHIBALD enters and starts to pack.

DR. CRAVEN. Archie, you *must* tell me what we are to do with Mary. She goes where she wants to go, and does what she wants to do. I cannot hope to succeed with Colin's treatment if she is allowed to sneak into his room and disturb him. You must send her away before she undoes everything we have tried to do.

ARCHIBALD. I can't send her away, Neville. She has no one on the earth but me. Can't you keep her outside? She likes the gardens, I believe.
DR. CRAVEN. What are you doing, Archie?
ARCHIBALD. I'm leaving, Neville. You have things well in hand here.
DR. CRAVEN. Well in hand? Haven't you heard anything I've just said?
ARCHIBALD. And last night, [MUSIC CUE #20: QUARTET] I dreamed I walked through the maze to Lily's garden, and saw Lily and Mary standing there. Mary, standing right there in Lily's garden. I turned away ... I couldn't watch ... I was afraid.
DR. CRAVEN.
WHY WON'T HE SAY WHAT HE WANTS,
WHY MUST HE SPEAK IN DREAMS?
WHY CAN'T HE SEE WHAT HE WANTS?
TO DISAPPEAR, IT SEEMS.

HE SHOULD SEND THIS HAUNTED GIRL FAR
    AWAY,
LEAVE THE HOUSE AND LANDS TO ME....

(ARCHIBALD continues his dream, IN SONG.)

ARCHIBALD.
I WATCHED THEM WALK AROUND THE GARDEN.
SHE STOOD TALL, GROWN STRONG AND BOLD.
THEN THEY TURNED, AND ASKED MY PARDON.
I COULDN'T SPEAK, MY HEART GROWN COLD.
DR. CRAVEN.
WHY CAN'T HE SEE WHAT HE WANTS?
HE WANTS THE PAST UNDONE.
WHY CAN'T HE KNOW WHAT HE WANTS?
HIS LOSING BATTLES WON.

TO HAVE NEVER LOVED HER,

NEVER KNOWN, HOW COMPLETE A LOSS CAN BE.

> IF SHE COULD DISAPPEAR
> HE'D START AGAIN,
> AND LIVE LIKE OTHER MEN.
> HE COULD BE HAPPY THEN.
>
> IF SHE WOULD DISAPPEAR
> HE COULD BE FREE,
> CUT OFF FROM PAIN AND LOSS,
> A BIT LIKE ME.

(LILY and ROSE appear.)

ROSE. You can't marry this Archibald. He's a gloomy miserable cripple who hides himself away in that horrible house. You've said it yourself, he can't believe you love him. And neither can I!

LILY. No one is asking for your approval, Rose.

ROSE. If you don't care what happens to you, think about your children. Do you want your children to be crippled as well?

LILY. I will marry him.

QUARTET

DR. CRAVEN.	ROSE.
I CAN ARRANGE WHAT HE WANTS.	DON'T DO THIS.
HE'S LEFT IT ALL TO ME.	DON'T WED HIM.
NOW HE CAN HAVE WHAT HE WANTS.	DON'T BED HIM.
UNFETTERED HE WILL BE.	DON'T DO THIS.
SET HIM FREE TO WANDER	SET HIM FREE ...

THROUGH THE
  WORLD.
LET HIM GO
HIS LONELY WAY.
ARCHIBALD.
AND THEN I LONGED
  TO JOIN THEM,
  KNOW THE
PEACE THEY FEEL,
  THEIR JOURNEY
  DONE.
THEN I WOKE, ONCE
  MORE WITHOUT
  HER,
KNEW I MUST
  WANDER ON AND ...

ON I GO.

LIFE TO FIND

THROUGH THE
  WORLD.
LET HIM GO
HIS LONELY WAY.
LILY.

NOW THAT I LOVE HIM

I WILL LIVE FOR HIM

LIVE JUST TO LOVE
  HIM.
ROSE.
I WON'T FORGIVE
  YOU,
WON'T SEE YOU LIVE
  THERE.
LILY, I SWEAR,
I'LL NEVER SEE YOU.

DR. CRAVEN.	**ROSE.**	**ARCHIBALD.**	**LILY.**
JUST TO DISAPPEAR IS TO BE FREE,			DO WHAT YOU WILL THEN, I'LL
CUT OFF FROM PAIN	CUT OFF FROM PAIN	CUT OFF FROM PAIN	NEVER LEAVE HIM
CUT OFF FROM PAIN			
I'LL HELP HIM	CUT OFF FROM PAIN	CUT OFF FROM PAIN	CUT OFF FROM PAIN
DISAPPEAR	NOW YOU MUST LEAVE HIM	DISAPPEAR	HOW CAN I LEAVE HIM?
AND START AGAIN,			

DR. CRAVEN.	ROSE.	ARCHIBALD.	LILY.
AND LIVE LIKE	YES, YOU MUST LEAVE HIM.		I'LL NEVER LEAVE HIM
OTHER MEN,	YOU MUST BELIEVE ME.	LEAVE LOSS	NOR E'ER DECEIVE HIM
HE COULD BE HAPPY THEN	LILY PROMISE.	BEHIND ME	ROSE, I PROMISED.
JUST TO DISAPPEAR	NOW YOU MUST LEAVE HIM.	LIVE UNSEEN,	NEVER TO LEAVE HIM
IS TO BE FREE.	YOU MUST BELIEVE ME.	DISAPPEAR	NO, I WON'T LEAVE HIM
DISAPPEAR	I AM THINKING	DISAPPEAR	I AM THINKING

ROSE/LILY.
OF THE CHILDREN
I AM THINKING OF THE CHILDREN
I AM THINKING OF THE CHILDREN
(*LILY and ROSE exit.*)

ARCHIBALD. I shan't be gone long. Perhaps just 'til the autumn.

DR. CRAVEN. And Mary?

ARCHIBALD. I'll write her a note from Paris.

DR. CRAVEN. You wouldn't be sending Mary away, Archie. Only giving her the education she deserves. I feel quite certain that Albert and Rose wouldn't want the girl to grow up just wandering around.

ARCHIBALD. Yes, I see. Well, then ... perhaps you should look into a few schools. Someplace she could learn to sing would be pleasant. I'll leave it all in your hands, Neville. Now, I'll go look in on Colin and...

DR. CRAVEN. Just see you don't wake him.

ARCHIBALD. In ten years have I ever awakened the boy?

DR. CRAVEN. I'll gather the staff so you can say good-bye.

ARCHIBALD. Oh, for God's sake, Neville. Just let me slip away. (*Then realizing he has been too sharp.*) I'm sorry. [MUSIC CUE #20A: THERE'S A MAN—Transition] Tell them ... (*And then he can't handle it.*) Tell them whatever you always tell them.

(*ARCHIBALD leaves and DR. CRAVEN is left standing there. The DREAMERS enter.*)

ALBERT
AND A MAN CAN DREAM
OF A SIMPLE LIFE,
HUSBAND, CHILD AND WIFE,
LOVE AND FAITH ALL ROUND.
HOLMES
THEN A MAN MUST WAKE,
STAND AND GREET THE DAY,
SEE WHAT COMES HIS WAY,
FEET UPON THE GROUND.
ALICE AND CLAIRE.
THERE'S A MAN WHOM NO ONE SEES.
THERE'S A MAN WHO LIVES ALONE.
THERE'S A HEART THAT BEATS IN SILENCE FOR
THE LIFE HE'S NEVER KNOWN.

SCENE 3
COLIN'S ROOM

ARCHIBALD enters, sits down beside Colin's bed, and opens a large book. His shoulder casts a rounded shadow on the walls. [MUSIC DUE #21: RACE YOU TO THE TOP FO THE MORNING]

ARCHIBALD. Now, let's see....

WHEN WE LEFT OFF LAST NIGHT,
THE HIDEOUS DRAGON
HAD CARRIED THE MAID TO HIS CAVE BY
    MOONLIGHT.
HE GNASHED HIS TEETH, AND BREATHED
    HIS FIRE,
THE HEATH QUAKED, AND WE TREMBLED
    IN FEAR.

I SAID, "SOMEONE MUST SAVE THIS
SWEET RAVEN HAIRED MAIDEN,
THOUGH SURELY THE COST WILL BE STEEP."
SO WE LADS ALL DREW LOTS,
OUR INSIDES TIED IN KNOTS,
AND I WON AND THE REST WENT TO SLEEP.

SO I PICKED UP MY STAFF,
AND I FOLLOWED THE TRAIL OF
HIS SMOKE TO THE MOUTH OF THE CAVE.
AND I BID HIM COME OUT,
"YEA FORSOOTH," I DID SHOUT,
"YE FOOL DRAGON BE GONE OR BEHAVE."

AND THEN UNDER MY BREATH,
I UTTERED A CHARM SAID
TO MAKE THE WORST FIEND BECOME KIND.
"KNAVES AND KNIGHTS OF DIRE PLIGHTS
NOW DIMINISH HIS SIGHTS,"
AND IT WORKED AND THE DRAGON WENT
    BLIND.

AND HE CHARGED OFF THE CLIFF
HOWLING MAD AND HE DIED AND THE
MAIDEN ACCEPTED MY RING.
AND THEN YOU CAME ALONG,
AND WERE BRAVE, BOLD AND STRONG,
AND IN THANKS EVERY NIGHT NOW I SING......

RACE YOU TO THE TOP OF THE MORNING.
COME AND SIT ON MY SHOULDERS AND
    RIDE.
RUN AND HIDE, I'LL COME AND FIND
    YOU,
CLIMB HILLS TO REMIND YOU, I LOVE
    YOU,
MY BOY AT MY SIDE.

NOW ANOTHER FOUL DRAGON'S
APPEARED, I MUST LEAVE YOU.
HE'S SCORCHING OUR LAND WITH HIS BREATH.
FROM HIS LAIR, THIS ONE TAUNTS ME,
HE DARES ME, HE HAUNTS ME.
ONCE AGAIN, WE MUST FIGHT TO THE DEATH.

WOULD TO GOD I COULD STAY
AND INSTEAD
SLAY YOUR EVIL DRAGON,
THIS BEAST WHO SITS HUNCHED ON YOUR
    BACK.
WOULD GOD I COULD WRENCH HIM
        AWAY FROM YOUR BED,
OR CUT OFF OR TEAR OFF HIS TERRIBLE HEAD,
COULD BREATHE OUT MY FIRE ON HIM
        TIL HE WAS DEAD,
OR BEG HIM TO SPARE YOU
        AND TAKE ME INSTEAD.

AS IT IS, I MUST LEAVE YOU
IN CARE OF MY BROTHER, THE
WIZARD WHO LIVES ON THE HILL.
WHO HAS PROMISED HIS ART
WILL SOON PIERCE THROUGH THE HEART
OF THIS DRAGON THAT'S KEEPING YOU ILL.

AND I KNOW THAT YOUR MOTHER,
GOD BLESS HER, WOULD WANT YOU

TO DO AS HE SAYS AND GROW STRONG.
AND YOU KNOW THAT AS SOON AS I CAN
I'LL RETURN, SO BE BRAVE SON, AND
KNOW THAT I LONG ...

TO RACE YOU TO THE TOP OF THE
MORNING.
COME AND SIT ON MY SHOULDERS AND
RIDE.
RUN AND HIDE, I'LL COME FIND YOU,
CLIMB HILLS TO REMIND YOU, I LOVE
YOU,
I LOVE YOU......
MY BOY AT MY SIDE.

(ARCHIBALD stands and exits. [MUSIC CUE # 21A:
MAZE TRANSITION] ROSE and ALBERT appear,
as the scene changes to the gardens.)

ALBERT.
COME ALONG LOVE, COME FLY AWAY,
FLY ALONG, COME ALONG, FLY AWAY HOME.
COME ALONG, LOVE, YOU'VE COME A LONG
WAY,
YOU'VE FLOWN ALL THE DAY,
COME FLY AWAY HOME.
ROSE.
IT'S A MAZE THIS GARDEN,
IT'S A MAZE OF PATHS,
MEANT TO LEAD A MAN ASTRAY.
ALBERT and ROSE.
TAKE A LEFT AND THEN
TURNING LEFT AGAIN'S
HOW A SOUL MAY FIND THE WAY.

SCENE 4
IN THE GREENHOUSE

MARY enters the greenhouse and sits down on a bench.
DICKON enters.

DICKON. Ay op. Hello there, Mary.
MARY. (*Clearly unhappy.*) Ay op. Hello there.
DICKON. But why are you in such a bad temper, Mary? Are ye weary of lookin' for the key?
MARY. No, no. I found the key.
DICKON. You did?

(SHE shows it to him.)

DICKON. So I see. You're weary of lookin' for the door.
MARY. I'm not weary, Dickon. I found the door too. The garden is dead.
DICKON. No.
MARY. It is. It's all dead.
DICKON. A lot of things what looks dead is just bidin' their time. Now you tell me exactly what you saw.

[MUSIC CUE #22: WICK]

MARY. It's cold and gray. The trees are gray, the earth is gray. And there's this clingy kind of haze over everything.
DICKON. Like a body were in a dream.
MARY. It's the most forgotten place I've ever seen. With loose gray branches looped all around the trees like ropes or snakes, and dead roots and leaves all tangled up on the ground. So still and cold.
DICKON. But did you take a look real close look at anything? Did you scrape away a bit of the bark and have a real look at anything? Mary, the strongest roses will fair thrive on bein' neglected, if the soil is rich enough.

They'll run all wild, and spread and spread til they're a wonder.

MARY. You mean it might be alive? But how can we tell?

DICKON. Oh, I can tell if a thing is wick.

MARY. (*Now truly excited.*) Wick! I've heard Ben say Wick.

DICKON.

WHEN A THING IS WICK IT HAS A LIFE ABOUT
  IT.
MAYBE NOT A LIFE LIKE YOU AND ME.
BUT SOMEWHERE THERE'S A SECRET STREAK
  OF GREEN INSIDE IT,
NOW COME AND LET ME SHOW YOU WHAT I
  MEAN.

WHEN A THING IS WICK IT HAS A LIGHT
  AROUND IT.
MAYBE NOT A LIGHT THAT YOU CAN SEE.
BUT HIDING DOWN BELOW A SPARK'S ASLEEP
  INSIDE IT,
JUST WAITING FOR THE RIGHT TIME TO BE
  SEEN.

> YOU CLEAR AWAY THE DEAD PARTS
> SO THE TENDER BUDS CAN FORM.
> LOOSEN UP THE EARTH AND
> LET THE ROOTS GET WARM.
> LET THE ROOTS GET WARM.

WHEN A THING IS WICK, IT HAS A WAY OF
  KNOWING
WHEN IT'S SAFE TO GROW AGAIN, YOU WILL
  SEE.
WHEN THERE'S SUN AND WATER SWEET
  ENOUGH TO FEED IT,
IT WILL CLIMB UP THROUGH THE EARTH A
  PALE NEW GREEN.

YOU CLEAR AWAY THE DEAD PARTS
SO THE TENDER BUDS CAN FORM.
LOOSEN UP THE EARTH AND
LET THE ROOTS GET WARM.
LET THE ROOTS GET WARM.

  COME A MILD DAY.
  COME A WARM RAIN.
  COME A SNOWDROP A COMIN' UP.
  COME A LILY, COME A LILAC.
  COME TO CALL,
  CALLIN ALL OF US TO COME AND
   SEE ...

MARY.
WHEN A THING IS WICK,
AND SOMEONE CARES ABOUT IT,
AND COMES TO WORK EACH DAY,
LIKE YOU AND ME,
(*Spoken.*) Will it grow?
DICKON.
(*Spoken.*) It will.
MARY.
THEN HAVE NO DOUBT ABOUT IT,
WE'LL HAVE THE GRANDEST GARDEN EVER
SEEN.
  MARY. Oh, Dickon, I want it all to be wick! Would
you come and look at it with me?
  DICKON. I'll come every day, rain or shine, if you
want me to. All that garden needs is us to come wake it
up.
  MARY. But Dickon, what if we save the garden and
then Uncle Archie takes it back, or Colin wants it?
  DICKON. Ay, what a miracle that would be. Gettin'
a poor crippled boy to see his mother's garden.
  DICKON and MARY.
YOU GIVE A LIVING THING
A LITTLE CHANCE TO GROW.

THAT'S HOW YOU WILL KNOW IF SHE IS
WICK, SHE'LL GROW.

SO GROW TO GREET THE MORNING.
FREE FROM GROUND BELOW.
WHEN A THING IS WICK
IT HAS A WILL TO GROW AND GROW.
  MARY.
COME A MILD DAY.
COME A WARM RAIN.
COME A SHOWDROP, A COMIN' UP.
COME A LILY, COME A LILAC.
COME TO CALL,
CALLIN' ALL THE REST TO COME
  DICKON and MARY.
CALLIN' ALL OF US TO COME,
CALLIN' ALL THE WORLD TO COME.....

*(DICKON and MARY hear the chirp of the ROBIN and
quickly gather plants from the greenhouse.)*

  DICKON.
I PROMISE THERE'S A SECRET STREAK OF
GREEN BELOW.
  DICKON AND MARY.
AND ALL THROUGH THE DARKEST NIGHTTIME,
IT'S WAITING FOR THE RIGHT TIME.
WHEN A THING IS WICK, IT WILL GROW.

(They exit.
[MUSIC CUE # 22A: RACE YOU/Transition]
ALICE appears and sings, as the scene changes.)

  ALICE.
SO HE PICKED UP HIS STAFF,
AND HE FOLLOWED THE TRAIL OF THE SMOKE
TO THE MOUTH OF THE CAVE.
AND HE BID HIM COME OUT,

"YEA, FORSOOTH," HE DID SHOUT,
"YE FOOL DRAGON, BEGONE OR BEHAVE."

SCENE 5
COLIN'S ROOM

*COLIN is throwing a terrible tantrum. MARTHA and a
NURSE are trying to calm him.*

COLIN. Stop looking at me! I hate you! You're
horrible and ugly, under that haystack you call your hair!
MARTHA. Master Colin, please. Nurse's only tryin'
to ...
COLIN. If she won't close her eyes when she's in
my presence, then I will have her fired. *(To the NURSE.)*
Go away! Go away! Go away!
MARTHA. Master Colin, please. Nurse's only tryin'
to bring you your supper.
MRS. MEDLOCK. *(Entering.)* Martha! What is
going on in here!
MARY. *(Enters.)* Isn't anybody going to stop that
boy ...?
MRS. MEDLOCK. *(As she sees MARY.)* She is
not to go near him, Martha. Those are the doctor's direct
orders.
MARTHA. What can it hurt, Mum? He likes Mary.
Let her have a go at it.
MRS. MEDLOCK. No, Martha.

*(And without waiting for approval, MARY runs over to
the bed.)*

MARY. Colin Craven, you stop that screaming!
COLIN. Get away from me!

MARY. I hate you! Everybody hates you! You will scream yourself to death in a minute and I wish you would!

COLIN. Get out of my house!

MARY. I won't! You stop!

COLIN. I can't stop! I felt a lump on my back. I'm going to die!

MARY. There is nothing the matter with your horrid back!

COLIN. I'm going to have a lump on my back like my father and die!

MARY. Martha! Come here and show me his back this minute.

MARTHA. I can't, Mary. He won't let me.

COLIN. Show her the lump!

(Now MARTHA pulls aside Colin's covers and bedclothes.)

COLIN. Now feel it!

(MARY feels his back.)

COLIN. There!

MARY. Where?

COLIN. Right there!

MARY. No! There's not a single lump there. Except backbone lumps and they're supposed to be there. *(And now she turns her own back to him.)* See. I have them too.

(MARY grabs his hand and puts it on her back. And then places his hand on his own back for comparison.)

MARY. See? There's no lump.

COLIN. *(Quietly.)* It's not there.

MARY. No, it's not.

COLIN. (*Sits up a little straighter. Looking slightly pleased.*) It's not there.
MARY. You were just mad at me for not coming back when I said I would. (*He doesn't answer.*) Weren't you.
COLIN. Maybe.
MARY. (*Calmly.*) You were and you know it.
MARTHA. I'll leave you two alone, I think. (*And she leaves.*)

(MARY opens a music box, determined not to speak to him until he apologizes.)

MARY. This is nice.

[MUSIC CUE # 22B: THIS IS NICE]

COLIN. (*Relents.*) I'm sorry I said all those things about sending Dickon away. I was just so angry when you wanted to be with him instead of me. And then when you didn't come back like you said you would ...
MARY. I was always coming back, Colin. I'm as lonely as you are. I was just late, that's all. It just took me longer than I thought because ...
COLIN. Because what?
MARY. (*Takes a moment.*) Will you promise not to tell if I tell you?
COLIN. I never had a secret before, except that I wasn't going to grow up.
MARY. I found your mother's garden.
COLIN. Do you mean a secret garden? I've dreamed about a secret garden.
MARY. It's been locked up out there, just like you've been locked up in here, for ten years. Your father doesn't want anybody in it. Only I found the key. And the other night, after Dr. Craven and Mrs. Medlock found us here together, I ran out into the storm, and found the door. And now Dickon and I are working on it every day, and you can come too and ...

COLIN. What does it look like?

MARY. Well, right now, there's this tangle of vines all over everything because nobody's been taking care of it, but Dickon says if we cut away all the dead wood, there'll be fountains of roses by summer.

COLIN. I never wanted to see anything like I want to see that garden.

MARY. You *must* see it. But they must never know where we're going or Ben says Dr. Craven will send me away.

COLIN. No, Mary.

MARY. (*Going on.*) Maybe William can take you outside in your wheelchair. Then, when nobody's looking, Dickon could push you through the maze to the garden.

COLIN. I can't go outside, Mary. I'll take a chill if I go. I'll get even worse.

MARY. No, you won't. You'll feel better.

COLIN. I can't, Mary. I'm afraid.

[MUSIC CUE # 22C: CHOLERA CHORD]

(LIEUTENANT WRIGHT and MAJOR HOLMES appear.)

COLIN. I've been in this bed for so long. And I don't want to die.

LIEUTENANT WRIGHT. Just one blacksnake and this girl.

MAJOR HOLMES. I'm afraid there's no one left. Sorry, miss.

COLIN. I want to grow up, Mary. So I can't get sick. I'd like to see the garden, really I would, but I can't.

(LIEUTENANT WRIGHT and MAJOR HOLMES exit.)

MARY. All right, then. We'll just keep working on it til you're *ready* to see it. And whenever that is, you just tell me, and I'll get William to ...

COLIN. You must come back tomorrow afternoon after you're through working, and have supper with me and tell me everything you've done.

MARY. I'd like that. Goodnight, then.

COLIN. Goodnight, Mary.

[MUSIC CUE # 23: COME TO MY GARDEN]

(MARY leaves and LILY appears from behind Colin's bed and sings.)

LILY.
COME TO MY GARDEN,
NESTLED IN THE HILL.
THERE I'LL KEEP YOU SAFE BESIDE ME.

COME TO MY GARDEN,
REST THERE IN MY ARMS,
THERE I'LL SEE YOU SAFELY GROWN AND ON
    YOUR WAY.

STAY THERE IN MY GARDEN,
WHERE LOVES GROW FREE AND WILD.
COME TO MY GARDEN,
COME, SWEET CHILD.

COLIN.
LIFT ME UP, AND LEAD ME TO THE GARDEN,
    WHERE LIFE BEGINS ANEW.
WHERE I'LL FIND YOU,
AND I'LL FIND YOU LOVE ME TOO.

COLIN.	**LILY.**
LIFT ME UP, AND LEAD	COME TO MY GARDEN.
ME TO THE GARDEN	
WHERE LOVE GROWS	REST THERE IS MY
DEEP AND TRUE.	ARMS.

WHERE I'LL TELL YOU   THERE I'LL
WHERE I'LL SHOW   SEE YOU
   YOU
MY NEW LIFE, I WILL   SAFELY GROWN AND
   LIVE FOR YOU.   ON YOUR WAY

I SHALL SEE YOU IN   I SHALL SEE YOU IN
   YOUR GARDEN.   MY GARDEN
AND SPRING WILL   WHERE LOVE GROWS
   COME AND STAY.   FREE AND WILD
LIFT ME UP AND LEAD   COME TO MY GARDEN.
   ME TO THE
   GARDEN.
COME, SWEET DAY.   COME SWEET DAY.....

(LILY embraces COLIN and night closes in around them.)

SCENE 6
IN THE MAZE - THE GARDEN

By lantern light, DICKON and MARTHA are seen moving through the gardens.

MARTHA. Oh, I shouldn't be doin' this. I'm like to be sent back to the scullery for this, and I don't like the scullery, Dickon. I don't know anyone who does.

[MUSIC CUE # 23A: TO THE NIGHT GARDEN –
Transition]

DICKON. No one'll be missin' you at this hour.
MARTHA. But if it's so dark, I can't even see where I'm goin', how'm I to hope to see what it is once I get there?

DICKON. I can't say. Perhaps it's only somethin' you're meant to hear.
MARTHA. But all I can hear is me own self talkin',
DICKON. Then perhaps, y'd best be still.

(MARY appears, pushing COLIN in his wheelchair.)

MARY. Dickon, is that you?
DICKON. Aye, it is, Mary. And Martha, too.

(MARTHA is overcome, seeing COLIN outside.)

MARTHA. Ay' dear lad.
COLIN. Martha, are you surprised to see me outside in the middle of the night?
MARTHA. That I am, Master Colin, but just now, you looked so much like your mother, it made my heart jump.
MARY. Martha, come look!
(And with that, DICKON takes over from MARY and wheels COLIN into:)

THE GARDEN

COLIN. It's my mother's garden. It is.
MARY. It's a secret garden. And we're the only ones in the world that want it to be alive.
DICKON. Ay, Colin. We'll have you walkin' about and diggin' same as other folk before long.
COLIN. But how can I? My legs are so weak, I'm afraid to ...
DICKON. *(Tracing a circle on the ground.)* There's a charm in this garden, Colin. [MUSIC CUE # 24: COME SPIRIT COME CHARM] And the longer you stay in it, the stronger you'll be.
COLIN. What kind of a charm?

(Suddenly, the FAKIR and the AYAH appear, and MARY begins to intone an Indian charm.)

MARY and FAKIR.
A' O JADU KE MAUSAM.
A' O GARMIYO KE DIN.
A' O MANTRA TANTRA YANTRA.
US KI BIRARI HATA'O.
COLIN. *(Stares at her in amazement.)* Where did you learn that?
MARY. I don't *know*. I didn't even know I *knew* it.
COLIN. Martha, do *you* believe in spells and charms?
MARTHA. That I do, Master Colin, and spirits and the Big Good Thing by whatever name you call it.
MARY. *(As surprised as anyone by this.)* Now I know where I heard it . I even know what it means.
COLIN. Go on, then.

(MARY does the INDIAN hand language as she speaks.)

MARY.
COME SPIRIT, COME CHARM.
COME DAYS THAT ARE WARM.
COME MAGICAL SPELL.
COME HELP HIM GET WELL.

(And then DICKON translates Mary's words into a Yorkshire sounding tune.)

DICKON.
COME SPIRIT, COME CHARM.
COME DAYS THAT ARE WARM.
COME MAGICAL SPELL.
COME HELP HIM GET WELL.

(And MARTHA picks up the Yorkshire version and sings:)

MARTHA.
COME SPIRIT, COME CHARM.
COME DAYS THAT ARE WARM.
COME MAGICAL SPELL.
COME HELP HIM GET WELL.

(And then the FAKIR and the AYAH chant, as MARTHA and DICKON sing:)

MARTHA, DICKON, LILY, & DREAMERS.	AYAH, FAKIR & MARY.
SPIRITS FAR ABOVE	A' O JADU KE
CHARMS ALOFT ON HIGH	MAUSAM.
SWEEP AWAY THE STORMS,	A' O GARMIYO
RUMBLING 'CROSS THE SKY.	KE DIN. MAU-
SPEED THE RISING SUN,	SAM
MAKE THE BREEZE TO BLOW.	KE DIN ...
BID THE ROBINS SING,	A' O.
BID THE ROSES GROW.	

(MARY begins to dance. COLIN, DICKON and MARTHA applaud. Then MARY dances to them, inviting them to join her.
Suddenly, a wilder spirit takes over, as MARY begins to whirl around.)

AYAH, MARY, FAKIR, OFFSTAGE WOMEN. AH ....AH .... AH ....AH ....

AYAH MARY/DRM	FAKIR SHAW.	CHANT II	DREAMER WOMEN.
		AH-HE HE-AH AH-HE HE-AH	
	AH ...	AH-HE HE-AH AH-HE HE-AH	AH ...
(Clap Clap)	...	AH-HE HE-AH AH-HE HE-AH	
	......	AH-HE HE-AH AH-HE HE-AH	AH...
OON-DA OON-DE		AH-HE HE-AH AH-HE HE-AH	
TAKA DIKA DINUM DIKA DAH	AH...	AH-HE HE-AH AH-HE HE-AH	AH ...
OON-DA OON-DE	......	AH-HE HE-AH AH-HE HE-AH	......
TAKA DIKA DINUM DIKA DAH	......	AH-HE HE-AH AH-HE HE-AH	AH ...
TAKA DIKA DINUM DIKA DIKA OON-DA	......	AH-HE HE-AH AH-HE HE-AH AH-HE HE-AH	(Scream.)
TAKA DIKA DINUM DIKA DIKA OON-DA	......	AH-HE HE-AH AH-HE HE-AH AH-HE HE-AH	
DA DEE		AH-HE HE-AH AH-HE HE-AH	AH...
DOON DIN	AH...	AH-HE HE-AH AH-HE HE-AH	
DA DEE DOON DIN	......	AH-HE HE-AH AH-HE HE-AH	

		CHANT II	MARY.
DA DEE DOON		AH-HE HE-AH	
DIN		AH-HE HE-AH	
AYAH	FAKIR		
MARY/DRM	SHAW.		
JADOO DA DEE	HEH...	AH-HE HE-AH	
DIKA DAH		AH-HE HE-AH	
JADOO DA DEE	YAH!	AH-HE HE-AH	
DIKA DAH		AH-HE HE-AH	
DA DIKA	HEH...	AH-HE HE-AH	JA
DADEE DIKA		AH-HE HE-AH	
DAH OONDE			
JA DIKA DIKA	YAH!	AH-HE HE-AH	DOO
DIKA DIKA		AH-HE HE-AH	
DIKA TA!			
(Scream.)	(Scream.)		KE

MARTHA & DICKON.
AH............

ALL.
AH.................

DREAMERS.
OONDA OONDEE
TAKA DIKA DINUM DIKA DAH
DA DIKA DA DEE DIKA DAH DOON DEE
MARTHA/DICKON/MARY. (*Spoken while DREAMERS ad-lib Indian Chants.*)
    Come Spirit, Come Charm
    Come Spirit, Come Charm
    Come Spirit, Come Spirit

MARTHA, DICKON, MARY/LILY	DREAMERS	AYAH, FAKIR
COME SPIRIT, COME CHARM	AH......	AH ......
COME DAYS THAT ARE WARM	......	......
COME MAGICAL SPELL	COME MAGICAL SPELL	......

COME HELP HIM   COME HELP HIM   ......
   GET WELL   GET WELL

ALL.
COME SPIRIT, COME CHARM
COME DAYS THAT ARE WARM
COME MAGICAL SPELL
COME HELP HIM GET WELL

DREAMERS	DREAMERS	LILY, ROSE, MARY, MARTHA, DICKON	AYAH, FAKIR
COME SPIRIT, COME CHARM	COME SPIRIT, COME CHARM	COME COME	JA-DU KE...
COME DAYS THAT ARE WARM	COME DAYS THAT ARE WARM	SPIRIT COME	......
COME MAGICAL SPELL	COME MAGICAL SPELL	COME COME	MAU SAM ...
COME HELP HIM GET WELL	COME HELP HIM GET WELL	SPIRIT COME	......
COME COME	COME SPIRIT, COME CHARM	COME COME	GARMI-YO...
SPIRIT COME CHARM	COME DAYS THAT ARE WARM	SPIRIT COME	......
COME MAGICAL SPELL	COME MAGICAL SPELL	COME MAGICAL SPELL	KE-DIN...

ALL.
COME HELP HIM GET WELL

(COLIN stands.)

    COLIN. Mary!
    MARTHA. Bless you, child.
    MARY. Colin. It worked! *(MARY runs up to steady him.)*

COLIN. I think the spell is working in the house too. (*A moment.*) Two nights ago, [MUSIC CUE # 24A: I AM WELL] when it was bright moonlight, I woke up and felt something filling the room and making everything so splendid. And I pulled the drape from my mother's picture, and there she was, her eyes looking right down at me, and something new started flooding through me, making me so proud, so strong ... so ... tall. (*A moment.*) I shall live forever and ever! I shall find out thousands of things. (*He takes another step.*) I want to give thanks to something, to anything that will listen. (*And another step.*) I'm well!

MARTHA. Mary, child, do you see what you've done?

(*But as MARY helps COLIN take his first steps, COLIN falls. COLIN then sees BEN, who has heard their voices and come to investigate.*)

COLIN. Who is that man? Go away!

(*MARY and DICKON help COLIN back into his chair.*)

MARY. Colin, it's Ben Weatherstaff, who tends the gardens.

COLIN. Weatherstaff! Do you know who I am?

BEN. (*Approaches.*) You're young Master Colin, the poor cripple, but Lord knows how you got out here.

COLIN. I'm not crippled!

BEN. Then what have you been doing, hidin' out and lettin' folk *think* you were a cripple. And half-witted!

COLIN. Half-witted!

(*MARY laughs, and COLIN gives her a stern look.*)

COLIN. Come here. I want to talk to you. And don't you dare say a word about this.

BEN. I'm your servant, as long as I live, young master.

COLIN. Did you know my mother?

BEN. That I did. I was her right-hand, round the gardens. Even now, I'm only kept on because she liked me. She said to me once, "Ben, if I'm ever ill or if I go away, you must take care of my roses." (*A moment.*) When she did go away, the orders was no one was to come in here. But I come anyway, 'til my back stopped me, about two year ago.

COLIN. I want to know how she died.

BEN. (*After a moment.*) She was sittin' right there, on that branch. And it broke and that started her laborin' with you, only the fall had hurt her back. Still she clung onto life 'til you were born and then she put you in your father's arms and died.

COLIN. Is that why he hates me?

BEN. I'm sure he doesn't hate you, lad.

MARY. He doesn't even know you. Wait 'til he finds out you can stand.

COLIN. I don't want him to know anything about this. I don't want anything said to him 'til I can walk. Do you promise?

BEN. It's gettin' to be a full time job, keepin' track of all the secrets around here.

COLIN. This is a serious matter. Mary. Take my hand. (*He extends his hand.*) Dickon. (*DICKON takes Colin's other hand.*) Martha. You too, Ben.

(*And they form a circle around him.*)

COLIN. Do you swear by the charm in this garden, that not one of you will mention this to my father until I am completely well?

(*And they swear. More or less in unison.*)

BEN. That I do.

DICKON. Ay, Colin. Nary a word.
MARTHA. Ay Colin.
MARY. I promise.
COLIN. Good, then. (*And he releases their hands.*)
MARY. So what do you want to see first?
COLIN. I want to see the roses. [MUSIC CUE # 25: A BIT OF EARTH – REPRISE] Show me where the roses will be.

(*And as they go off to look at the roses, ALBERT, LILY and ROSE appear.*)

LILY.	ROSE.	ALBERT.
		A BIT OF EARTH
A BIT OF EARTH		A DROP OF DEW
	A BIT OF EARTH	A SINGLE STEM BEGINS
BEGINS TO RISE		TO RISE
		THAT BIT OF EARTH IS PUSHED AWAY THE FLOWERS BLOOM BEFORE OUR EYES
BEFORE OUR EYES	BEFORE OUR EYES	
		FOR IN THE EARTH A CHARM'S AT WORK THE WORD IS PASSED

	THE DAYS ARE WARM
THE DAYS ARE WARM	

THE DAYS ARE
  WARM

                    THE DAYS ARE   UNFOLD AND
                      WARM   GROW
                                      THE WINTER'S
                                        PAST

WE'RE FREE   WE'RE FREE
  FROM   FROM
  HARM   HARM
                    WE'RE FREE
                      FROM
                      HARM
A BIT OF   A BIT OF   A BIT OF
  EARTH   EARTH   EARTH
A BIT OF   A BIT OF   A BIT OF
  EARTH   EARTH   EARTH

SCENE 7
THE LIBRARY

DR. CRAVEN and MRS. MEDLOCK are in the library awaiting the arrival of the headmistress from the school they have selected for Mary. DR. CRAVEN is in an uncharacteristically good humor.

DR. CRAVEN. Well, Mrs. Medlock. What a fine morning this has turned out to be.
MRS. MEDLOCK. Yes, doctor.
DR. CRAVEN. I trust this headmistress will be quite impressed, riding cross the moor on such a day. Perhaps she could even join me for tea I daresay she might relish a bit of civilized conversation, living as she does, in the company of spinsters and orphaned girls.

(MRS. MEDLOCK is somewhat offended by that remark, but doesn't remark on it.)

MRS. MEDLOCK. I'm sure she would be quite flattered by your attention, sir.

(JANE, a housemaid, appears with MRS. WINTHROP.)

JANE. Beg pardon, doctor. It's Mrs. Winthrop, sir. *(JANE exits.)*
DR. CRAVEN. Yes, Madam. Come in. Do come in. Please.
MRS. WINTHROP. Good day, Doctor.
DR. CRAVEN. And this is our housekeeper, Mrs. Medlock.
MRS. WINTHROP. How do you do?
DR. CRAVEN. I trust you had a pleasant journey.
MRS. WINTHROP. Actually, not. I have always found scenery, by itself, to be quite tiresome.
DR. CRAVEN. Well, then, you will be relieved to find we have contrived to keep all the scenery outdoors. Won't you sit down. *(Taking the forms from his jacket.)* I've completed all the forms you sent us, and I think you'll see my brother has included a contribution to the school's building fund. You didn't request it, of course, but as I told my brother, I'm sure you're in the planning stages of something or other. *(Then to MRS. MEDLOCK.)* Mrs. Medlock, will you see what's keeping Mary?

(MARY enters, followed by FAKIR and AYAH.)

MARY. I'm right here, sir.
DR. CRAVEN. Quite right. Here's our girl. *(Making the intro.)* Mary Lennox, this is Mrs. Winthrop, of the Abeerdeen School for Girls.
MRS. WINTHROP. Good morning, Mary.
MARY. I don't want to go to a school.

MRS. WINTHROP. Oh, but you do. A useless child never knows her worth, we say.

MARY. My Uncle Archibald said ...

DR. CRAVEN. Perhaps if you would tell Mary a little about the school, she'd see she there is no reason to be ...

MRS. WINTHROP. Certainly. And let me say from the start that you are not on trial here. The Board of Trustees has accepted your application.

DR. CRAVEN. Oh ... That's good news, indeed.

MARY. I won't go. You can't make me! (*MARY throws a cookie on the floor.*)

DR. CRAVEN. Mary Lennox!

MRS. WINTHROP. That's all right, doctor. This is exactly the type of behavior we are best equipped to handle.

[MUSIC CUE # 26: MARY'S TANTRUM]

MARY. My Uncle Archibald is the only one who says where I'm going to go and he says I don't have to go to any stupid school!

DR. CRAVEN. She's just frightened, I'm sure. Children are quite often depressed after a tragedy such as she has suffered.

(*MRS. WINTHROP forces MARY to pick up the cookie.*)

MRS. WINTHROP. Of course, doctor. Perhaps she would enjoy seeing some photographs of the girls at their work. I've brought several samples of the fine lace for which our girls are so ...

MARY. I hate you! You're a horrible, ugly pig ...

DR. CRAVEN. That's quite enough, young lady!

MARY. Your school is a filthy rathole full of brats and dirty beds. And all anybody really does there is scrub floors! (*She takes a breath.*) I hope you get hit by a lorry

on the way home and your ugly head rolls off in a ditch and gets eaten by maggots! (*Another breath.*) I hate you! I hate you! I hate you! And if I'm sent off with you, I'm going to bite your arm and you're going to die! Get out of here! (*She throws a chair.*)
MARY. Go away! Go away! Go away!
MRS. WINTHROP. Well, we have had one or two cases of this severity. (*MARY stamps on MRS. WINTHROP'S foot.*)
DR. CRAVEN. Mary Lennox!

(*MARY launches into a full-blown tantrum, cursing in Hindi as the AYAH and the FAKIR make menacing signs and native droning sounds upstage.*)

MARY.	[Translation]
Mar jaa>o	[Die]
Baarh me jaa>o	[Go drown yourself in the flood]
Chhoro mujhe!	[Leave me alone]
Tum barii shaitaan ho!	[You're a big devil]
Mar jaa>o!	[Die!]

(*MARY finishes by whirling around and falling to the floor, feigning unconsciousness.*
MRS. WINTHROP picks up her purse and papers.)

MRS. WINTHROP. Doctor, what you have here, is a medical problem.

(*MRS. WINTHROP exits. FAKIR and AYAH follow and with MARY feeling quite proud of herself, DR. CRAVEN looks down at the girl.*)

DR. CRAVEN. I'll speak with Mary alone, Medlock.
MARY. (*Gets up and curses him again.*) Chhoro mujhe! I'm going outside.

DR. CRAVEN. (*Grabbing her.*) You're going wherever *I* send you, young lady, and right this moment it's into that chair.

MARY. Uncle Archibald said I didn't have to go to a school.

DR. CRAVEN. Oh for God's sake. He doesn't care about you. All he wants is never to see you again. Why do you think he left without even saying goodbye to you?

MARY. Maybe he was in a hurry.

DR. CRAVEN. You drove him away. You remind him of his wife.

MARY. I look like my Aunt Lily?

DR. CRAVEN. Now it is my task to find you a suitable place to go so that my brother can return. The next school I will contact will send no representative. Your bags will be packed and you will leave Saturday week.

MARY. But I can't leave now. Colin needs me.

DR. CRAVEN. The last thing the boy needs is you. Another month of trying to keep up with you and we'll have to put him in hospital, or worse.

MARY. No, you won't. He's much better.

DR. CRAVEN. You have no idea how ill he is. When Colin was born, the midwife didn't expect him to live a week. But I, have kept the boy alive for ten years. Only now, thanks to you, he is in grave danger of relapse.

MARY. But you haven't seen how ...

DR. CRAVEN. Do you want him in hospital? Do you want him to die?

MARY. To die?

DR. CRAVEN. Yes! To die. If Colin is too active at this stage in his recovery, if you push him to take his first step too soon, before his heart is strong enough, he will not survive it. Do you understand, Mary? Colin's very life is in your hands.

(And suddenly, LIEUTENANT WRIGHT and MAJOR HOLMES appear.)

DR. CRAVEN. One moment, he would be chatting away, and the next moment, he would sink to the ground and die.
MARY. And die?
DR. CRAVEN. Yes! You *have* choices in your life. Colin does not. I will not see the boy in hospital for the rest of his life, or dead before his life even begins. You must go, and go you will. Now that is all I have to say to you.

(MARY cannot answer. But she doesn't leave.)

DR. CRAVEN. Why are you standing here? Are you quite amused to learn of your power?
MARY. I didn't do anything. You locked him in his room.
DR. CRAVEN. You may go.
MARY. You don't want Colin to get well at all. You want him to die so you can have this house.

(Suddenly, almost out of control, DR. CRAVEN raises his arm, as though to hit MARY. [MUSIC CUE #27: DISAPPEAR – TRANSITION] Then he stops himself.)

DR. CRAVEN. *(Screaming.)* You will leave Saturday week!

(MARY runs from the room, and DR. CRAVEN sings.)

DR. CRAVEN.
THERE'S NOTHING HERE THAT I WANT.
HOW DARE SHE MAKE THIS CLAIM?
ISN'T IT CLEAR WHAT I WANT?
TO SERVE HAS BEEN MY AIM.

STILL, I HAVE TO WONDER
WHO I'D BE,
IF IT ALL BELONGED TO ME.

IF THEY'D ALL DISAPPEAR,
I'D START AGAIN.
I COULD BE HAPPY THEN,
I'D LIVE LIKE OTHER MEN.

IF THEY'D ALL DISAPPEAR,
I COULD BE FREE.
CUT OFF FROM PAIN AND LOSS,
AT LAST, I'D BE.

SCENE 8
MARY'S ROOM

As MARTHA packs some of Mary's clothes, she tries to comfort the girl.

MARTHA. Mary, you had *nothing* to do with your uncle's leaving. It weren't you child. Your uncle liked you, I know he did. Didn't he tell you you could have a garden? Didn't he send you clothes and bring you books? Well, didn't he?

MARY. But Colin's going to die and it's all my fault.

MARTHA. And what have you done for Colin except get him goin' outside every day, and get him eatin' his food and gettin' him believin' he can get strong again? I think you were just what Colin needed.

MARY. But you're not a doctor, Martha. Will you tell him I'm sorry. I mean, after I'm gone, will you tell him I didn't mean to hurt him, that I didn't want to go?

MARTHA. I think you better tell him that yourself.

MARY. I can't, Martha. He'll just get mad and start acting all high and mighty. And then Dr. Craven might send him away, too.

MARTHA. You're talkin' like you're already gone, Mary.

MARY. I *am* gone, Martha. I wish I were a ghost.

MARTHA. No ghost [MUSIC CUE #28: HOLD ON] could do what you've done in this house, Mary. *(Singing.)*

WHAT YOU'VE GOT TO DO IS
FINISH WHAT YOU HAVE BEGUN.
I DON'T KNOW JUST HOW,
BUT IT'S NOT OVER TIL YOU'VE WON.

WHEN YOU SEE THE STORM IS COMIN',
SEE THE LIGHTNING PART THE SKIES.
IT'S TOO LATE TO RUN,
THERE'S TERROR IN YOUR EYES.
WHAT YOU DO THEN IS REMEMBER
THIS OLD THING YOU HEARD ME SAY,
IT'S THIS STORM, NOT YOU,
THAT'S BOUND TO BLOW AWAY.

    HOLD ON,
    HOLD ON TO SOMEONE STANDIN' BY.
    HOLD ON,
    DON'T EVEN ASK HOW LONG OR WHY.
    CHILD, HOLD ON TO WHAT YOU KNOW IS
      TRUE,
    HOLD ON TIL YOU GET THROUGH.
    CHILD OH CHILD....
    HOLD ON.

WHEN YOU FEEL YOUR HEART IS POUNDIN',
FEAR A DEVIL'S AT YOUR DOOR.
THERE'S NO PLACE TO HIDE,
YOU'RE FROZEN TO THE FLOOR.
WHAT YOU DO THEN IS YOU FORCE YOURSELF

TO WAKE UP AND YOU SAY,
IT'S THIS DREAM NOT ME
THAT'S BOUND TO GO AWAY.

    HOLD ON,
    HOLD ON THE NIGHT WILL SOON BE BY.
    HOLD ON,
    UTNIL THERE'S NOTHIN' LEFT TO TRY.
    CHILD, HOLD ON, THERE'S ANGELS ON
       THEIR WAY.
    HOLD ON AND HEAR THEM SAY,
    CHILD OH CHILD.......

       AND IT DOESN'T EVEN MATTER,
       IF THE DANGER AND THE DOOM
       COME FROM UP ABOVE, OR DOWN
          BELOW,
       OR JUST COME FLYIN' AT YOU
       FROM ACROSS THE ROOM.

WHEN YOU SEE A MAN WHO'S RAGIN',
AND HE'S JEALOUS AND HE FEARS
THAT YOU'VE WALKED THROUGH WALLS
HE'S HID BEHIND FOR YEARS,
WHAT YOU DO THEN IS YOU TELL YOURSELF
TO WAIT IT OUT, YOU SAY,
IT'S THIS DAY, NOT ME, THAT'S
BOUND TO GO AWAY.

       CHILD, HOLD ON ...
       IT'S THIS DAY, NOT YOU
       THAT'S BOUND TO GO AWAY.

MARY. What do you think I should do?

MARTHA. I think you should find a pen and paper and write to your uncle in Paris and tell him to come home. I think you should let Colin's father say whether he likes him standin' or not.

MARY. But why would he listen to me? And what if the letter didn't get to him in time?

MARTHA. I'm sure your uncle will send for you as soon as he sees what you've done for the boy. (*Getting the paper.*) Now here's some paper, and here's a pen. You do know how to write, I hope. 'Cause I won't be much help to you in that department.

MARY. A little.

MARTHA. That's all right. You don't have much to say, do you.

(MARY begins to write.)

[MUSIC CUE #29: LETTER SONG]

MARY.
D-E-A-R.....
.........UNCLE   ARCHIE,

(ARCHIBALD appears in PARIS, reading the letter.)

MARY.
HOW ARE YOU? I'M FINE.
EVERYBODY ELSE IS TOO.
PLEASE COME HOME.

ARCHIBALD. Home, I have no home.

MARY.
MARTHA SAYS THAT YOU'RE IN PARIS.
IS THAT VERY FAR AWAY?

ARCHIBALD. It's a house, child. Just a house.

MARY.
DO THEY HAVE NICE GIRLS AND BOYS THERE?

ARCHIBALD. And I can't get far enough away from it.

MARY.
PLEASE COME HOME.

MARTHA. Now just sign it ...

(MARY looks up a moment, wondering what else she should put in the letter.)

MARY.
SHOULD I SAY THAT COLIN'S WELL NOW?
ARCHIBALD.
—STREETS OF PARIS LIKE A MAZE.
MARY.
SHOULD I SAY THAT DOCTOR CRAVEN—
ARCHIBALD.
—SLEEPLESS NIGHTS AND AIMLESS DAYS.
MARTHA.
I THINK THAT WHAT YOU HAVE IS GOOD.
LET'S GET IT POSTED, ON ITS WAY.
HE'LL RUSH HOME, THEN YOU CAN TELL
HIM ALL THE REST YOU HAVE TO SAY.

MARY.	**ARCHIBALD.**
OH KIND SIR,	
UNCLE ARCHIE	…CAN'T FORGET,
HOW I WISH THAT	CAN'T EAT OR SLEEP
YOU COULD SEE	OR LIVE …
WHEN YOU COME	
INTO THE GARDEN	
PLEASE, COME HOME	…CAN'T FORGIVE …

MARY.
YOURS TRULY?
MARTHA. Well, maybe …
MARY.
SINCERELY?
MARTHA. Well, how about …
MARY.
YOUR FRIEND, MARY.

SCENE 9
PARIS

[MUSIC CUE #30: WHERE IN THE WORLD]

THE STAGE is empty except for a cloudy backdrop.
ARCHIBALD stands alone.

ARCHIBALD.
NOW I SEE YOU IN THE WINDOW
OF A CARRIAGE, THEN A TRAIN.
STILL MY MIND WILL NOT ACCEPT THAT
IN YOUR GRAVE YOU MUST REMAIN.
NOW I HEAR YOUR VOICE, THEN TURN AND
SEE A STRANGER'S FORM AND FACE.
MUST I WANDER ON TORMENTED
PLACE TO PLACE TO PLACE TO PLACE.

WHERE CAN I GO THAT YOU WON'T FIND ME?
WHY CAN'T I FIND A PLACE TO HIDE?
WHY DO YOU WANT TO CHASE ME, HAUNT ME?
EVERY STEP YOU'RE THERE BESIDE ME.

WHERE IN THE WORLD, TELL ME WHERE
IN THE WORLD
CAN I LIVE WITHOUT YOUR LOVE?
WHERE ON THE EARTH, TELL ME WHERE
ON THE EARTH
CAN I STAY NOW THAT YOU ARE GONE?

WHY DID I HAVE TO MEET YOU, LOVE YOU?
WHY CAN'T I RID YOU FROM MY MIND?
WHY DID YOU HAVE TO WANT ME, WON'T YOU
LET ME PUT MY LIFE BEHIND ME?

HOW IN THE WORLD, TELL ME, HOW IN THE
WORLD
CAN I LIVE WITHOUT YOUR LOVE?

WHY ON THE EARTH, TELL ME, WHY ON THE
    EARTH
SHOULD I STAY NOW THAT YOU ARE GONE?
NOW...THAT YOU ARE......

(Suddenly, LILY appears.)

   ARCHIBALD. Lily? Is that you?

   [MUSIC CUE #31: HOW COULD I EVER KNOW?]

   LILY.
HOW COULD I KNOW I WOULD HAVE TO LEAVE
    YOU?
HOW COULD I KNOW I WOULD HURT YOU SO?
YOU WERE THE ONE I WAS BORN TO LOVE.
OH, HOW COULD I EVER KNOW?
HOW COULD I EVER KNOW?

(ARCHIBALD walks over to sit down at his desk.)

   LILY.
HOW CAN I SAY TO GO ON WITHOUT ME?
HOW WHEN I KNOW YOU STILL NEED ME SO?
HOW CAN I SAY NOT TO DREAM ABOUT ME?
HOW COULD I EVER KNOW?
HOW COULD I EVER KNOW?

FORGIVE ME,
CAN YOU FORGIVE ME?
AND HOLD ME IN YOUR HEART.
AND FIND SOME NEW WAY TO LOVE ME,
NOW THAT WE'RE APART....

*(She approaches him, and finally moves to touch him, her
    hands caressing his shoulders.)*

LILY.
HOW COULD I KNOW I WOULD NEVER HOLD
YOU?
NEVER AGAIN IN THIS WORLD, BUT OH,
SURE AS YOU BREATHE, I AM THERE INSIDE
YOU.
HOW ... COULD I EVER KNOW?
HOW COULD I EVER ...?
  ARCHIBALD. (*He turns to sing directly to her.*)
HOW CAN I HOPE TO GO ON WITHOUT YOU?
HOW CAN I KNOW WHERE YOU'D HAVE ME GO?
HOW CAN I BEAR NOT TO DREAM ABOUT YOU?
HOW CAN I LET YOU GO?
  LILY.
HOW COULD I EVER KNOW?

(The music picks up the melody from the waltz in the first act.)

  ARCHIBALD.
ALL I NEED IS—
  LILY.
—IS THERE IN THE GARDEN
  ARCHIBALD.
ALL I WOULD ASK IS—
  LILY.
IS CARE FOR THE CHILD OF—
  LILY and ARCHIBALD.
—OUR LOVE.
  LILY.
COME, GO WITH ME.
SAFE I WILL KEEP YOU.
  ARCHIBALD.
WHERE YOU WOULD LEAD ME,
THERE I WOULD,
  LILY.
THERE I WOULD, THERE WE WOULD

ARCHIBALD and LILY.
THERE WE WILL GO....

(ARCHIBALD stands as LILY pulls him to her. They embrace and sing, their forgiveness complete, their love gloriously renewed and real.)

ARCHIBALD AND LILY.
HOW, HOW COULD I KNOW.
TELL ME HOW, HOW COULD I KNOW.
EVER TO KNOW YOU WILL NEVER LEAVE ME.
HOW COULD WE EVER KNOW?
　　ARCHIBALD.　　　　　**LILY.**
HOW COULD I EVER
　　KNOW?

　　　　　　　　　COME TO MY GARDEN

(LILY takes ARCHIBALD by the hand and leads him offstage.)

[MUSIC CUE # 32: TO THE DAY GARDEN]

SCENE 10
THE DAY GARDEN

It is morning. VOICES are heard from offstage.

COLIN. Mary! What is it?

(DICKON and MARTHA appear.)

DICKON. Mary! Come quickly!
MARY. Wail til you see it!

(MARY wheels COLIN into the garden.)

COLIN. Mary, what is it?
MARY. It's spring!
COLIN. But where did it come from?
DICKON. From all our hard work, where do you think?
COLIN. Everything is so ... Look at it!
MARY. But where's Ben? He has to see what's happened.
MARTHA. I'll go and fetch him. (*MARTHA exits to look for BEN.*)
DICKON. Colin, look at the lilacs....

(*DICKON wheels COLIN round and round in the wheelchair.*)

DICKON.
COME SPIRIT, COME CHARM.
COME DAYS THAT ARE WARM.
COME GATHER AND SING,
AND WELCOME THE SPRING.

MARY and COLIN.	**DICKON.**
	COME
COME	SPIRIT, COME
COME	CHARM, COME
SPIRIT, COME CHARM	DAYS THAT ARE
	WARM

MARY, COLIN and DICKON.
COME GATHER AND SING
AND WELCOME THE SPRING
COLIN. Mary, look at the roses!
MARY. There *are* fountains of them!
COLIN.
Mary, Mary, quite contrary,
How does your garden grow?

(*MARY grabs Dickon's staff and taunts Colin in return.*)

MARY. I'm not contrary. You take that back.
COLIN. You make me!

(DICKON wheels COLIN offstage, chased by MARY.)

MARY. (*Unseen.*) I will! I've got you, Colin Craven.

(And suddenly, LILY leads ARCHIBALD and DR. CRAVEN into the garden.)

DR. CRAVEN. Archie, why didn't you cable us you were coming.
ARCHIBALD. I didn't know, myself, Neville.

(DR. CRAVEN hears the sounds from inside the garden: the CHILDREN shrieking with delight.)

DR. CRAVEN. What on earth is all that noise?
COLIN. (*Unseen.*) Oh no you don't. I'm lots faster than you. Here we come!

(COLIN pushes MARY, who is now in the chair, into the garden.)

MARY. Colin Craven, not so fast!
DR. CRAVEN. Mary Lennox!

(COLIN stops as he sees his father and DR. CRAVEN.)

COLIN. Father!

(ARCHIBALD can't believe what he sees.)

COLIN. Look at me! (*Crosses slowly to his father.*) I'm well!
ARCHIBALD. (*Clasps the boy to him.*) Oh, Colin, my fine brave boy. Can you ever forgive me?

COLIN. It was the garden that did it, Father, and Mary and Dickon, and some kind of ... charm that came right out of the ground.

ARCHIBALD. Neville, were you hoping to surprise me with this news?

DR. CRAVEN. I knew they were looking better, but I had no idea they were ...

COLIN. We didn't want you to know. We were afraid you wouldn't let us come to the garden if you knew.

DR. CRAVEN. But how did you—

COLIN. William carried me down the stairs until—

DR. CRAVEN. But what have you eaten? You haven't touched the food we've sent to your rooms for weeks.

COLIN. Martha sent us food, we ate in the garden. We ate enough for ten children.

ARCHIBALD. You did, did you.

COLIN. Oatcakes and roasted eggs and fresh milk and—

DR. CRAVEN. It was all terribly confusing. After all these years, to—

ARCHIBALD. It was confusing, Neville. Why don't you take my flat in Paris and stay as long as you like. And when you return, perhaps you will allow me to help you re-establish your practice, in town if you like, so you can resume your own life, free of the enormous burden you have carried on our behalf.

DR. CRAVEN. Thank you, Archie.

MARY. (*To ARCHIBALD.*) And will you stay home with us?

ARCHIBALD. Colin, Colin. Look at you.

COLIN. It was Ben that kept the garden, alive, Father, until we could get here.

BEN. I knew it was against your orders, sir, but—

ARCHIBALD. As I remember, it was Lily who ordered you to take care of this garden, Ben. Well done.

BEN. Thank you, sir.

COLIN. And it was Dickon who—
ARCHIBALD. Yes. I can imagine. Dickon if there is every anything we can—
MARTHA. (*Interrupts him.*) Sir. What is to become of our Mary?

[MUSIC CUE #33: FINALE]

ARCHIBALD. Why, Mary.
ALBERT.
CLUSTERS OF CROCUS...
MARY. Here's your key, if you want it back, sir. You didn't bury it after all. I'd have never found it if you ...
ARCHIBALD. I had nearly forgotten you in all this.
MARY. (*Bravely.*) It's hard to remember everybody, sir.
ARCHIBALD. No it isn't. Three isn't very many people at all. I should be able to remember three people quite easily.
MARY. (*Carefully.*) Would I be one of them?
ARCHIBALD. Mary Lennox, for as long as you will have us, we are yours, Colin and I. And this is your home. And this, my lovely child ... (*He opens his arms.*) is your garden.

(*MARY rushes into his embrace and he holds her close as DICKON and MARTHA clasp hands. THE DREAMERS approach, singing, then take their leave of MARY, one by one.*)

DREAMERS.
COME TO MY GARDEN,
NESTLED IN THE HILL.
THERE I'LL KEEP YOU SAFE
BESIDE ME.
COME TO MY GARDEN.
REST THERE IN MY ARMS.

THERE I'LL SEE YOU
SAFELY GROWN AND ON YOUR WAY ...

(ROSE exits.)

LILY AND ALBERT.
STAY HERE IN THE GARDEN,
AS DAYS GROW LONG AND MILD.

(ALBERT exits.
Then finally, MARY, COLIN, stand together, with
ARCHIBALD kneeling between them, as LILY sings.)

LILY.
COME TO THE GARDEN.
COME, SWEET CHILD.

(LILY blows them a final kiss. We hear a single
GLISSANDO and she disappears.)

THE END

COSTUME PLOT

Mary Lennox
#1
Off-white muslin nightgown w/lace
Off-white leather slippers
#2
Black on black woven print challis dress/w taffeta and
  lace collar and cuffs
Black hose
2 pc. white cotton knit knicker & camisole
Black high-top shoes
Black wool coat w/cape; deep purple velvet trim
Black taffeta & deep purple velvet muff
Black velvet hat w/ribbon trim
#3
Light rust print challis dress w/off-white lace trim
Black hose
Rose & gray wool plaid coat w/woven braid trim
Knitted cap w/pom-pom
Knitted scarf
Brown high-top shoes
#4
White pique nightgown w/eyelet trim
Persimmon wool knit cardigan
Off-white leather slippers
#5
Bottle green challis dress w/collar
Black hose
Black high-top shoes
#6
Embroidered white cotton batiste dress w/lt. blue silk
  unders
White hose
White high-top shoes
White straw hat w/flowers & ribbon
#7
White percale nightgown w/lace neckline & border

Olive green knit cardigan
#8
Purple linen houndstooth dress w/lace insets
Pink floral pinafore w/ruffle
Black hose
Black high-top shoes
#9
Peach chiffon floral dress w/lace
Mint green chiffon pinafore w/peach taffeta sash, silk
  nosegays
White hose
Straw hat w/pink ribbon
White high-top shoes

Lily
#1
Lavender organza & chiffon tea dress w/floral neckline
Mauve organza petticoat
Mauve hose
Off-white high-button shoes
Pearl necklace w/pearl medallion
Pearl drop earrings
#2
3/4 Coral floral chiffon garden dress
Yellow/pink cotton floral apron
Crepe de chine petticoat
Dusty pink straw hat w/ribbon
Cameo
Pearl earrings
Low-heeled, off-white high-button shoes
White hose
#3
Lavender/gray silk, silver lace net ball gown w/glass &
  sequin embroidery
Gray organza petticoat w/silver lace
Ribbon & floral hair ornament
Amethyst & crystal drop necklace
Crystal drop earrings

Gray hose
Lavender silk slipper w/bow
#4
White cotton & lace afternoon dress w/lavender silk
    unders
White batiste petticoat
White straw hat w/veil
White hose
Off-white high-button shoes
Broach
Pearl earrings
White lace gloves

Rose
#1
Sequin embroidered organza & peach silk ball gown
Ivory organza petticoat
Ivory silk 16-button gloves
Peach hose
Dusty rose brocade slipper w/rose ornament
Floral headdress w/feather
Cameo earrings
Pearl, crystal, & cameo necklace
Lace shawl
Lace edged lawn handkerchief
#2
3/4 Dusty rose print chiffon garden dress
Crepe de chine petticoat
Yellow/peach & slate blue cotton floral apron
Straw hat w/horsehair & ribbon trim
Pettipoint broach
Pearl earrings
Low-heeled, ivory high-button shoes
Ivory hose
#3
White eyelet, long-sleeved, afternoon dress w/coral silk
    unders
White cotton batiste petticoat

White lace gloves
White hose
Ivory high-button shoes
White straw hat w/veil & cherry blossoms
Pearl earrings
Broach
Pearl necklace

Alice
#1
Embroidered organza & lavender silk ball gown w/floral trim
Ivory organza petticoat
Lavender floral, feather headdress
Ivory satin 16-button gloves
Ivory hose
Lavender brocade slippers
Lavender glass & pearl necklace
Pearl & gold earrings
Lace shawl
Floral fan
#2
White eyelet afternoon dress w/yellow silk unders
White cotton batiste petticoat
White hose
Ivory high-button shoes
Pale yellow straw hat w/horsehair trim
Crochet lace gloves
Broach
Pearl earrings
Necklace
White lawn parasol w/battenburg lace, yellow silk lining

Claire
#1
Embroidered organza & net, pink/gold silk ball gown
Ivory organza petticoat
Lt. peach hose

Pale gold brocade slippers
Ivory satin 16-button gloves
Pearl cluster & drop earrings
Topaz crystal & pearl necklace
Floral & crystal hair ornament
Lace shawl
#2
White eyelet & lace inserted batiste afternoon dress
    w/light pink silk unders
White cotton batiste petticoat
White hose
Ivory high-button shoes
White straw hat w/veil & flowers
Lace gloves
Pearl earrings
Pearl necklace
Pearl bracelet
Broach

Ayah
#1
Off-white silk saree
Silk short-sleeved top
Silk pongee pants
Hat w/saree border
Gold & pearl drop earrings
India print canvas slippers
#2
White silk saree w/pink & gold bullion border
White silk w/gold bullion short sleeve top
White silk w/gold bullion pants
Hat w/pink & gold bullion border
Gold & pearl drop earrings
White & gold brocade slippers

Mrs. Medlock
#1
Black wool coat w/high collar

Lace & pleated black wool cape
Black leather gloves
Black felt hat w/bow
Black hose
Black leather & suede high-button shoes
2
Charcoal gray wool dress w/white pique collar, cuffs
Gray cotton petticoat
Black hose
Black leather & suede high-button shoes
Black & maroon crocheted wool shawl
Pendant watch
Black onyx & gold drop earrings
3
Green/gray paisley woven shawl
4
White eyelet afternoon dress w/coffee silk unders
White cotton batiste petticoat
White cotton gloves
Ivory straw hat w/flowers
Enameled broach
Antique gold drop earrings
White hose
Ivory high-button shoes
5
Slate blue challis & lace blouse
Charcoal gray wool skirt
Gray cotton petticoat
Black hose
Black leather & suede high-button shoes
Pewter drop earrings
Broach
Eyeglass on chain
Gray/green paisley woven shawl
6
Mauve print blouse w/tucking
Dark taupe striped wool skirt w/belt
Tan cotton petticoat

Black hose
Black leather & suede high-button shoes
Beige woven shawl
Broach
Drop earrings

Martha
#1
Gray, blue & black wool plaid dress w/lace collar & cuffs
Natural cotton petticoat
Lt. tan cotton pinafore
Black hose
Black laced boots
Oatmeal wool sweater
#2
Beige stripe dress w/lace collar & cuffs
Lt. beige cotton petticoat
Dove gray shadow stripe cotton pinafore w/lace
White hose
Tan laced boots
Straw hat
#3
Green & taupe plaid dress w/crochet lace collar
Natural cotton petticoat
Black hose
Black laced boots
Lt. tan cotton pinafore

Maids
Gray wool gabardine dress w/pique collar & cuffs
Ivory cotton petticoat
White & gray stripe bib apron w/lace insert
Black hose
Black Gigi boots
White on white plaid cotton dust cap w/lace

Mrs. Shelley
Plum velvet coat w/3 cord embroidery

Lambs wool & plum velvet muff
Gray leather gloves
Plum velvet hat
Black hose
Black Gigi boots
Gold, amethyst drop earrings

Female Dancers
#1
Gray/green organza, pink & silver net, sequin
    embroidered ball gown w/net drape
Pearl gray organza petticoat
Long satin glove
Gray hose
Gray green brocade slipper w/sequin trim
Crystal & floral hair ornaments
Pink crystal necklace
Pink crystal earrings
#2
Blue organza, blush & silver lace, sequin embroidered
    ball gown w/net drape
Pearl gray organza petticoat
Long satin gloves
Gray hose
Slate blue brocade slipper
Lt. amethyst & crystal necklace
Lt. amethyst & crystal earrings
Floral hair ornaments

Mrs. Winthrop
Taupe green wool suit w/taupe velvet collar & trim
Gray & white stripe blouse w/bow
Black hose
Lt. gray cotton petticoat
Black Gigi boots
Tortoise shell glasses
Silver pin
Silver drop earrings

Stripe taffeta parasol
Taupe leather gloves
Black purse

Nurse
Dark charcoal & white stripe dress w/white collar & cuffs
Off-white cotton petticoat
White lawn pinafore w/buckle
White lawn cap w/ruffle
Black hose
Black Gigi boots

Archibald Craven
#1
Brown herringbone wool frock coat w/faille lapels
Matching trousers
Brown double-breasted wool vest w/green wool notched
   collar
Cream on cream stripe shirt w/detachable collar, French
   cuffs
Gold cufflinks
Watch, watch chain
Silver taupe & deep rust paisley cravat
Stick pin
Brown hose
Brown Wellingtons
Olive wool Inverness coat
Olive felt hat
Brown silk suspenders
#2
Maroon & olive woven paisley double-breasted smoking
   jacket w/fringed sash
Brown herringbone wool trousers
Brown double-breasted wool vest w/green wool notched
   collar
Cream on cream stripe shirt w/detachable collar, French
   cuffs

Gold cufflinks
Watch & watch chain
Silver taupe & deep rust paisley cravat
Stick pin
Brown hose
Brown Wellingtons
#3
2 pc. brown stripe sack single-breasted suit
Olive single-breasted vest
Ivory cotton shirt w/detachable straight point collar,
    French cuff
Enameled cufflinks
Gold watch & watch chain
Green/taupe tapestry brocade tie
Brown & green silk suspenders
Brown hose
Brown Wellingtons
Olive wool Inverness coat
Olive felt hat
Walking stick
#4
4-button single-breasted white wool sack coat
Single-breasted white wool w/blue pinstripe vest
White wool w/blue pinstripe trousers
Lt. blue cotton shirt w/white club collar & French cuffs
Gold cufflinks
Gold watch & chain
Lt. yellow chavet silk tie
Mother of pearl stick pin
White socks
Oyster leather plain cap toe brogues
Straw boater w/yellow/blue ribbon
#5
Brown wool check single-breasted vest & trousers
Tan & fawn stripe cotton shirt w/neckband & French
    cuffs
Burgundy, ochre, dk. taupe wool challis brocade
    dressing gown w/notched lapel

Burgundy & gold cord belt w/tassels
Brown socks
Brown Wellingtons
Gold watch & chain
Gold cuff links
 # 6
Pale loden gray 3 pc. sack suit, single-breasted vest
   w/notched lapel
Off-white cotton shirt w/detachable straight point collar
   w/pin, French cuff
Loden tie w/gold tan figure
Gold stick pin
Gold cuff links
Gold collar pin
Gold watch & chain
Loden socks
Green taupe high laced shoes
Gray silk suspenders

Dr. Craven
 # 1
3 pc. charcoal gray glen plain single-breasted sack suit,
   w/ single-breasted vest w/notched collar
Blue/white stripe shirt w/white cotton detachable stand
   collar French cuffs
Purple/navy floral brocade tie
Gray silk suspenders
Silver stick pin
Silver & enamel cuff links
Silver watch & watch chain
Black socks
Black high-top shoes
Pewter metal frame glasses
 # 2
Charcoal gray glen plaid vest & trousers
Blue/white stripe shirt w/white cotton detachable stand
   collar; French cuff
Purple/navy floral brocade tie

Gray silk suspenders
Silver stick pin
Silver & enamel cuff links
Silver watch & watch chain
Black socks
Black high-top shoes
Pewter metal frame glasses
Forest green & pumpkin wool challis brocade dressing
   gown w/forest green satin shawl w/2-tone cord trim

#3
Dk. charcoal wool flannel double-breasted frock coat;
   vest w/black braid trim
Black/white check wool trousers
White cotton w/blue shadow stripe shirt w/detachable
   club collar, French cuffs
Black w/cream & purple figure silk cravat
Black silk suspenders
Silver cuff links
Silver stick pin
Silver watch w/watch chain
Black socks
Black Wellingtons
Pewter metal frame glasses

#4
Dk. charcoal wool flannel vest w/black braid trim
Black & white check wool trousers
White cotton w/blue shadow stripe shirt w/detachable
   club collar, French cuffs
Purple silk tie
Black silk suspenders
Silver stick pin
Silver watch w/watch chain
Black socks
Black Wellingtons
Pewter metal frame glasses
Dk gray/blue cable knit wool cardigan w/shawl collar

5
Off-white w/gray pinstripe silk Norfolk jacket
Off-white silk herringbone double-breasted vest &
   trousers
Lt. blue & white stripe cotton shirt w/straight point collar,
   French cuffs
Lt. blue silk tie
Off-white silk suspenders
Enamel cufflinks
Silver stick pin
Silver watch & watch chain
White socks
Champagne leather Wellingtons
Straw boater w/2-tone blue ribbon

6
3 pc. L. gray Glen plain single-breasted suit w/single
   breasted vest w/ notched lapel
Lt. gray stripe cotton shirt w/straight point collar &
   French cuffs
Lt. gray /blue silk tie w/diamond pattern
Gray silk suspenders
Silver cuff links
Silver stick pin
Silver watch & watch chain
Black socks
Black laced high-tops
Pewter metal frame glasses

Captain Albert Lennox
1
Honey wool twill British army uniform coat w/off-white,
   gold braid
Matching trousers w/gold/off-white side stripe
Faded rose silk sash w/tassels & 3 medals
White leather sword belt w/gold buckle
Captains' insignia

Tan socks
Honey brown high-top boots
White gloves
Tan suspenders
#2
Lt. cream wool gabardine British army uniform coat
  w/off-white & gold braid
Matching trousers with gold/off-white side stripe
White leather sword belt w/gold buckle
Captains' insignia
White socks
Ivory leather Wellingtons
White cotton gloves
White suspenders

Major Holmes
#1
Honey wool twill British Army uniform coat w/off-white
  & gold trim
Matching trousers w/gold & off-white side stripe
Peach/beige silk sash w/tassel
White leather sword belt w/gold buckle
Majors' insignia
Cream suspenders
Tan socks
Honey brown high-top boots
White cotton gloves
#2
Four-pocket khaki drill w/off-white trim
Matching wool trousers
Brown belt
Majors' insignia
Khaki socks
Dk. brown Wellington
Khaki helmet w/off-white band
#3
Lt. cream gabardine British army dress uniform coat
  w/off-white & gold trim

Matching wool trousers w/gold & off-white side stripe
White leather sword belt w/gold buckles
Majors' insignia
White suspenders
White socks
Ivory leather Wellingtons
White cotton gloves

Lt. Shaw
#1
Honey wool twill British army dress uniform coat w/off-
    white & gold trim
Matching wool trousers w/gold & off-white side stripe
Peach/beige silk sash w/tassels
White leather sword belt w/gold buckle
Lieutenants' insignia
Cream suspenders
Tan socks
Honey brown high-top boots
White cotton gloves

#2
Lt. cream wool gabardine British patrol jacket w/matching
    braid & buttons
Matching wool trousers
White suspenders
Lieutenants' insignia
White socks
Ivory leather Wellingtons
White cotton gloves
White forage cap w/gold trim

Lt. Wright
#1
Honey wool twill British army dress uniform coat w/off-
    white & gold trim
Matching wool trousers w/gold & off-white side stripe
Peach/beige silk sash w/tassels

White leather sword belt w/gold buckle
Lieutenants' insignia
Cream suspenders
Tan socks
Honey brown high-top boots
White cotton gloves
#2
Four-pocket khaki drill w/off-white trim
Matching wool trousers
Brown belt
Lieutenants' insignia
Khaki socks
Dk. brown Wellingtons
Khaki helmet w/off-white band
#3
Lt. cream wool gabardine British patrol jacket w/matching
   braid & buttons
Matching wool trousers
White suspenders
Lieutenants' insignia
White socks
Ivory leather Wellingtons
White cotton gloves
White forage cap w/gold trim

Fakir
#1
Tan, cream & peach woven silk coat w/burnt peach,
   brown, cream cotton sash
Peach silk trousers
Black, red, blue, gold, cream patterned stripe drape
Tan cotton turban
Cream leather slippers
#2
Peachy tan & cream floral saree silk coat w/peach silk
   sash
White on white woven silk trousers
White/gold saree silk drape

White/peach silk turban
Peach & gold brocade slippers

Extra Fakirs
Yellow/cream raw silk coats w/wooden buttons
Tan/white raw silk sash
Raw silk trousers
Wool felt hat
Olive canvas slippers

Ben
#1
Heathered olive plaid wool rustic coat
Olive, tan & maroon plaid wool challis peasant shirt
   w/collar band
Stained tan canvas trousers
Old leather apron
Leather suspenders
Green knitted scarf
Knitted cap
Wool gloves
Lt. green & gold print handkerchief
Brown socks
Brown high-top shoes
#2
Oatmeal pebbled linen coat
Gray & brick on white tattersall cotton peasant shirt
   w/point collar
Brown plaid ribbon tie
Oatmeal herringbone linen trousers
White leather apron
Off-white suspenders
Panama hat w/brown band
Off-white socks
Natural desert boots
#3
Brick/tan plaid cotton peasant shirt w/collar band

Loden & gray green houndstooth long wool vest w/patch
   pockets
Dirty tan canvas trousers
Leather suspenders
Knitted cap
Lt. green & gold print handkerchief
Brown socks
Brown high-top shoes

Dickon
#1
Gray, black & white cotton flannel plaid shirt w/collar
   band
Off-white knitted underwear top
Green/gold cotton print neck scarf
Sheepskin long vest
Aged tan linen trousers
Maroon suspenders
Maroon knitted puttee's
Brown laced shoes
Brown/green wool cap
Walking stick
#2
Brick, lt. blue on white stripe cotton shirt w/neck band
Honey & ivory linen plaid vest w/braid trim
Off-white linen trousers
Oatmeal knit puttee's
Off-white suspenders
White socks
Taupe high top laced shoes
Taupe/off white tweed cap
#3
Pale olive & black cotton plaid shirt w/collar band
Taupe/brown wool vest w/collar
Aged tan linen trousers
Maroon suspenders
Maroon knitted puttee's
Brown laced up shoes

Brown/green wool cap

Colin
#1
Cream w/blue pinstripe oxford cloth night shirt w/white
  cotton collar
#2
Ivory wool gabardine sailor suit w/lt. blue/white cord and
  trim
Matching knickers
White hose
White high-top shoes
White straw hat
White suspenders
#3
Blue/gold on white tattersall cotton night shirt w/white
  cotton collar
Beige/ivory wool blanket
#4
Off-white gabardine shawl collar jacket w/mint
  green/white stripe trim
Pink/white cotton pinstripe shirt w/Eaton collar
Peach silk taffeta bow
Mint green silk houndstooth knickers
White hose
White suspenders
White high-top shoes
Natural straw hat w/gray/green ribbon edge

Major Shelley
Navy melton double-breasted British army great coat
Navy forage cap w/gold trim
Black leather riding boots
Black leather gloves

Porter
Black/gray wool herringbone coach jacket
Gray & mauve knitted wood scarf

Dark taupe w/multi color flecked wool knickers
Dark over the knee hose
Black laced high-tops
Dark wool tweed cap

Male Waltzers
Slate gray wool gabardine 2 pc.. tail suit w/peaked lapel
Ice gray & silver brocade vest w/collar
White pique front cotton shirt w/detachable wing collars
White pique square end bow tie
White suspenders
Pearl gray studs & cuff links
Gray hose
Gray leather pumps w/grosgrain bow
White cotton gloves

Butlers
Gray wool flannel swallow tail coat w/brown velvet
   upper collar
Matching trousers
Black & tan cotton stripe single-breasted vest
White pique front cotton shirt w/detachable stand collar
Black barathea four in hand tie
Pewter cuff links
Black suspenders
White cotton gloves
Black socks
Black Wellingtons

PROPERTY PLOT

I-OP
Small framed photograph of Lily (Mary)
Red, weighted man's handkerchief (Fakir)
7 Red silk man's handkerchiefs (Fakir, Shaw & Alice;
    Wright, Holmes, Claire)
Riding crop (Wright)
Candelabra (Neville)
Candle holder (Archie)
Mary's doll & dress (Betsy)
Mary's passport & visa (Shelley)
2 Red silk man's handkerchiefs (Albert & Ayah)
Japanese fan (Alice)
Luggage checks (Timothy)
Torch candle (William)
India bed w/pillow (onstage)
Mary's settee (turntable on/off)
Mary's trunk w/coat, scarf, hat, shoes, socks (Timothy
    (T/T off)
Ottoman (Jane (T/T off)
Doll's house w/doll attached
Cart with luggage (Timothy on/off)
Mary's tea table (Turntable on/off)
Rockinghorse (William)

I-1
Mary's doll & dress (Betsy)
Breakfast tray (bowl of porridge, 2 spoons, tea
    cup/saucer, creamer, sugar bowl, napkin (Martha)
Jump rope (long length) (Martha)
Mary's settee (Turntable on/off)
Mary's trunk w/coat, scarf, hat, shoes, socks (Timothy
    (T/T off)
Ottoman (Jane (T/T off)
Mary's tea table (Turntable on/off)
Rockinghorse (William)

I-2
Lily's picture (Mary)
Jump rope (short length) (Mary)

I-3
Jump rope (short length) (Mary)
Lily's picture (Mary)
Pots, spritzer, small clippers (on planter)
Dickon's stick (Dickon)
Wheelbarrow (w/pots), clippers, pruners, 2 sacks of dirt,
    small trowel (Ben)
Metal key to garden door (on Robin topiary)
Peacock topiary (Wright/Fakir)
Swan topiary (Holmes)
Greenhouse w/bench & table
Greenhouse w/2 tables
Robin topiary (Shaw)
Owl topiary (Albert)
Bench

I-4
Decanter of water, glass, documents, globe w/monkey,
    books
Blotter, inkwell, fountain pen, leases, architectural plans,
    unfolded documents, ruler, compass
Long stem red rose (Albert)
Archie desk (William/Timothy on/off)
Side chair (Betsy on/off)
Desk chair (Jane on/off)
Armchair, side table, bust & loose books

I-5
Armchair, side table, bust & loose books
Hall bench (Betsy–Fakir off)

I-6
Plastic garden key/candle (Mary)
Candle (Martha)

Hall bench (Betsy–Fakir off)

I-7
Wheelchair w/blanket (Betsy on/off)
Doctor's bag (w/syringe, vial) (Neville)
2 Large pillows, 2 laced pillows & support pillows
Red picture book, 2 books; music box
Colin's bed (William/Timothy)

I-8
5 Red silk man's handkerchiefs
   (Holmes/Claire/Alice/Fakir/Shaw)
3 Red silk man's handkerchiefs (Ayah/Rose/Wright)
Robin topiary (Jane)
Owl topiary (William)
Swan topiary (Betsy)
Peacock topiary (Timothy)

ACT II

II-1
Picnic basket (Rose/Lily)
2 Cups/saucers/spoons (Rose/Lily)
Small pink book (Lily)
Wicker tray w/tea pot & 2 cups/saucers/spoons/creamer &
   sugar (Archie/Albert)
White rose (Archie)
Red rose (Albert)
White blindfold (man's hanky) (Mary)
2 Badminton rackets (Martha & Ayah)
Camera on tripod w/off-white cape (Holmes)
Flash for camera (Holmes)
Parasol (Alice)
Red weighted man's handkerchief (Neville)
Wicker wheelchair (Medlock)
Large birthday cake w/candles (Ben)
Wicker tea cart (Fakir off)
2 Wicker chairs (Albert/Ayah off)

II-2
3 Books/Lily photo/music box/cylinders/Lily's scarf
Shaving kit (Archie)
Brushes/brush case/collars/collar box/trunk key
Drawer w/books/periodicals/3 other books
Table (Jane/Betsy T/T off)
Chaise (William/Timothy T/T off)
Steamer trunk

II-3
Large story book (Betsy)
Japanese fan (Alice)
Colin bed w/o side tables (William/Timothy on/off)
Bedroom chair (Betsy on/off)

II-4
Plastic garden key (Mary)
Dickon's stick (Dickon)
10 pots
Robin (Alice/Shaw)
Swan topiary (Holmes)
Greenhouse w/bench & table
Greenhouse w/2 tables
Peacock topiary (Fakir/Wright)
Owl topiary (Claire)

II-5
Dinner tray (Betsy)
Music box
Colin's bed w/SR table (William)

II-6
Outdoor lantern (Martha)
Dickon's stick (Dickon)
Outdoor lantern (Ben)
Wheelchair w/blanket (Mary/Colin)

II-7
Parasol (Winthrop)
Leather folder w/lace hanky (Winthrop)
Binoculars/leather folder w/documents & signed check
Tea service (2 pots/cups/saucers/spoons/plate of cookies
    one of which can be thrown/sugar bowl/pitcher of milk)
Archie desk & chair (T/T on/off)
2 Side chairs (one must be thrown) (T/T on/off)
Tea table (T/T on/off)
Armchair w/pillow (T/T on/off)

II-8
Tablet w/stationery/fountain pen
3 Books
Open suitcase w/3 pieces of clothes/doll
Letter (Archie)
Shroud/short jump rope (on rockinghorse)
Mary's settee (T/T on/off)
Tea table (T/T on/off)
Ottoman (T/T on/off)
Rockinghorse (William)

II-9
Lily photo/Lily scarf/3 books/pen/inkwell
Paris desk/backless chair/luggage stand w/suitcase

II-10
Wheelchair (Mary/Colin)
Dickon's stick (Dickon)
Plastic garden key (Mary)